Kyle fel ⸻ ⸻ ⸻ ⸺ ⸺ his eyes

Annie stood in front of him, her lip trembling. He rose, mere inches from her.

"It's Auntie G." She paused, as if unable to go on. "They're...hospitalizing her. Dehydration, the doctor said. And other complications. Fluid buildup and..."

He couldn't help himself. He reached for her. "I'm so sorry."

A sob choked her and she pressed herself into his arms, dampening his shirtfront with her tears. "Oh, Kyle, what am I going to do?"

He held her in his embrace, breathing in her floral scent, thinking of all that had happened between the two of them. It didn't matter. None of it did. Because he knew the answer to her question. *This*. Simply and inevitably *this*.

Dear Reader,

Recently I spent a week with our youngest grandchild. Eight years old, she told me, "Nana, I want to be an author." As we chatted about writing, I suggested that every story needs to give a sense of place and every protagonist should undergo a positive change. She was off and running, filling pages with the fruits of her fertile imagination.

A Letter for Annie came from several trips to Oregon. The ruggedly beautiful Pacific Coast inspired the setting of this book. As for change in the main characters? Initially, Annie is simply marking time in her life. When circumstances force her to return to Eden Bay, she is not prepared to meet former classmate Kyle Becker. Remembering how Annie broke his best friend's heart, Kyle resents her presence.

Good storytelling involves a journey that betters the main characters, and good romances focus on the redeeming power of love. I hope you will find both Annie and Kyle become better people and deserve the love they share.

Enjoy,

Laura Abbot

P.S. I always appreciate hearing from readers. You may write me at P.O. Box 373, Eureka Springs, AR, 72632-0373, or at LauraAbbot@msn.com.

A LETTER FOR ANNIE
Laura Abbot

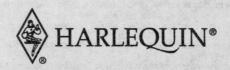

TORONTO • NEW YORK • LONDON
AMSTERDAM • PARIS • SYDNEY • HAMBURG
STOCKHOLM • ATHENS • TOKYO • MILAN • MADRID
PRAGUE • WARSAW • BUDAPEST • AUCKLAND

Recycling programs
for this product may
not exist in your area.

ISBN-13: 978-0-373-71555-8
ISBN-10:   0-373-71555-2

A LETTER FOR ANNIE

www.eHarlequin.com

Printed in U.S.A.

Books by Laura Abbot

HARLEQUIN SUPERROMANCE

Don't miss any of our special offers. Write to us at the following address for information on our newest releases.

Harlequin Reader Service
U.S.: 3010 Walden Ave., P.O. Box 1325, Buffalo, NY 14269
Canadian: P.O. Box 609, Fort Erie, Ont. L2A 5X3

For our talented, motivated and loving grandchildren.
You give us constant joy, fill us with pride and promise us a hopeful future.
May your lives be forever blessed.

PROLOGUE

Afghanistan
Early 2003

BORED AND CHILLED, Sergeant Kyle Becker huddled in the driver's seat of the Humvee, watching a watery sun sink behind the rugged, snow-covered peaks. As soon as the guys finished securing the last pontoon of the river crossing, they could head out of this godforsaken wilderness back to base. They'd been lucky this time. No Taliban guerrillas harassing them. No toothless mountain men glaring at them or big-eyed children begging for chocolate. Just another friggin' mission.

The first of the Guard engineers loaded their gear and climbed in. The rest followed quickly. Kyle turned on the ignition so they could hightail it as soon as the stragglers were aboard. Pete brought up the rear. He opened the passenger door to ride shotgun, then paused and reached into the pocket of his parka.

"Save it, Nemec." Kyle revved the motor. "We're getting the hell out. Now."

"Just one peek while it's still light." Pete turned his head to get a better look at the photograph of a smiling girl with reddish-brown hair and soulful hazel eyes. It took only a fraction of a minute. One fraction too long.

Before any of the Guardsmen could react to the movement behind the rock, Pete lay on the ground, blood from a temple wound pooling in the dirty snow.

"Shit!" Heart thundering, Kyle slid from the truck, shouldered his weapon and crawled to his friend's side. There was no sign of the sniper, a crumpled body the only evidence he had ever been there.

With his lifeless buddy's head resting against his shoulder, the drive back to base seemed interminable.

CHAPTER ONE

Eden Bay, Oregon
Early April, 2009

FOG VEILING the rugged Oregon headlands and an angry ocean were unmistakable omens: *Turn back. You don't have to do this.* Ignoring her internal voices, Annie Greer pulled in front of her great-aunt Geneva's seaside cottage and sat for a long moment in her battered Honda, gathering herself to face what lay ahead.

Only Auntie G. could have compelled Annie to return to the town she'd fled a decade earlier. Out of the blue the call had come to Bisbee, Arizona, where she earned her living waiting tables and creating individually crafted handbags. On the day she celebrated her first sale to a pricey boutique in Scottsdale, the telephone had shattered her euphoria. Carmen Mendoza's summons had been brief and urgent. "Your *tia* Geneva, she has put off asking me to call. But now I think I must. She has not so long. I am with her, of course. But I am not family. She should not die without family. She has only you. Please to come home."

A gull shrieked overhead, and Annie gathered her

windbreaker closer to ward off a sudden chill. *Home.* She snorted. Once, Eden Bay had been exactly that. Once, she had imagined a future here. But on a cloudless May night ten years ago, her dreams—and her innocence—had died swiftly, mercilessly. She had hoped never to set foot in Eden Bay again, never to confront painful memories.

However, she couldn't turn away from her great-aunt Geneva, now that the elderly woman was suffering from congestive heart failure. Not after all Geneva had done in those days when Annie had desperately needed to hide where no one from this town could ever find her. Although Carmen had been her aunt's faithful caregiver and companion for years, she was right. She wasn't family.

Only Annie was family.

After the death of Annie's mother the summer following her junior year in high school, Auntie G. had become Annie's sole living relative. Even so, because of Geneva's frequent world travels, they had seen little of each other in the past few years. It would be good to share this precious time.

Annie continued staring at the cottage, fending off memories that filled her with shame.

Finally, knowing Auntie G. needed her, she opened the car door and stood gazing at the roiling ocean, licking sea salt from her lips. She loved her great-aunt, but returning to Eden Bay was the second most difficult decision she had ever made in her life.

GENEVA GREER SPREAD the afghan over her legs and adjusted the nosepiece of her portable oxygen tank. She had been reluctant to uproot Annie, but the truth was, Geneva didn't want to depart this world without seeing her great-niece again. Without making one more attempt to help Annie come to terms with the past.

Glancing around the room, she hoped Annie would find solace in the familiarity of the Greer family beach house. The fireplace with its hand-crafted mantel and built-in wood box, the brass telescope on the window ledge, the ship's model on top of the bookcase—all of these things had been here since Geneva's father built the Cape Cod–style cottage in the mid-1930s. Some of her happiest childhood memories were of carefree days with her younger brother, running wild on the beach, wading into the surf, studying marine life in the tide pools.

Now the house was nearly as weathered as Geneva. The railing on the front porch was dangerously loose and a water stain marred the ceiling in one of the upstairs bedrooms. She wondered what Annie would think of her legacy. Whether it would tether her to Eden Bay. Or provide her with the means of leaving the place behind, once and for all.

Lost in her thoughts, she roused at the sound of a car door slamming. In years past, she would have raced out to greet her beloved great-niece. Now, she could only wait.

Peering through the window, Geneva feasted her eyes on Annie, whose shoulder-length auburn hair stirred in the wind. Her pale, freckled face, unadorned with makeup, reminded Geneva so much of her own long-dead brother. Dressed in jeans, a shapeless maroon windbreaker and purple Crocs, Annie paused, shading her eyes with her arm to look toward the sea. Then with a resolute lift of her shoulders, she turned and walked toward the house, rearranging her expression from wistfulness to welcome.

Geneva sighed. Annie was home. But pain, she knew, would dog her niece's every step. She shouldn't have summoned her. Selfish old woman.

If only…if only she didn't need her so.

OPENING THE DOOR, Carmen engulfed Annie in a warm hug. "It is good you are here," she said, before standing aside. Annie set down her backpack and stood silently, soaking it all in.

First came the familiar smells—musty books, lemon oil, bread fresh from the oven. Then the sights—the brass umbrella stand, the ornate upright piano that had belonged to her grandmother and Geneva's easel, splotched with every color of the rainbow. Annie took a deep breath, propelled into a time when this house had been a happy place, her sanctuary.

"Annie?" The voice was faint, raspy, anxious. Nothing like the lilting alto she remembered. Carmen nodded toward the bay window facing the ocean.

Moving into the room, Annie found her great-aunt huddled beneath a multicolored afghan. Auntie G. had always been vibrant, larger than life. Her robust laughter, expansive gestures and bohemian clothing had made her, for Annie, the most exotic and beloved of creatures. She forced a smile so as not to betray her shock, then knelt beside the pale husk of a woman engulfed by the chair she had once dominated. "Auntie G., I'm so happy to see you." Annie struggled to control her voice. "I've missed you."

"And I you, petunia."

Use of the pet name melted away the years, and for a fleeting moment, Annie could feel her father's arms hoisting her over his head. *Touch the sky, my little petunia.*

Geneva rested a frail hand on Annie's hair. "I didn't want to ask this of you."

"I know. But you're worth it."

"Maybe it's time you came back anyway." Geneva fingered the fringe of her afghan. "It's hard work burying the past, but it needs to be done."

I don't want to talk about this. Please, not now. "I doubt that's possible. Anyway—" Annie projected a cheerfulness she did not feel "—I'm here for you, not me."

"The point is to make the most of every moment. I want time with you, but we have to be realistic. It won't last long."

Annie buried her face in her aunt's lap, silent tears falling on the afghan. When she raised her head, her voice broke. "I need you. I can't face this place by myself."

"You can and you will, with or without me."

Despairing, Annie had no answer. Like a diabolical metronome, the oxygen tank ticked off Geneva's breaths. Annie fought the impulse to run to her car, throw it in gear and race far away. Yet, if not for her great-aunt, where in God's name would she be now?

Stark raving mad, probably. The automatonlike life she'd lived since leaving this town was safer. At least in Arizona she'd been able to keep memory at bay. If only she could barricade herself in this house that had once sheltered her. Simply be with Geneva. Not let anyone else know she'd returned.

"Tea?" Carmen entered holding a tray with a cup of tea and homemade brownies.

Annie rose, took the tray and settled in the cane-bottomed rocker across from Geneva. "Thank you," she said, struggling to smile at Carmen. "I forgot about lunch, so this is a welcome snack."

"Save room for dinner. My special enchilada casserole. Maybe we can tempt Señorita Geneva." Carmen's brown eyes signaled her concern.

Annie studied her aunt. "Aren't you eating?"

Geneva waved her hand dismissively. "I'm on a diet." She managed a chuckle. "All my life I've wanted to be svelte. A pity I had to wait until now."

Annie appreciated the attempt at humor. Still, Carmen had not exaggerated the severity of Geneva's condition. Annie took a sip of tea, mentally vowing to set aside her own pain to alleviate Geneva's. But was that possible here in Eden Bay?

"DAMN IT TO HELL." Kyle Becker stood on the roof of the Brady place, staring at the half-assed job the roofer had done. No wonder it leaked. Shoddy workmanship and shortcutting on materials. Kneeling, he pried up a layer of shingles and cursed again. What was so hard about doing a job right? But then, if everyone did a perfect job, he'd be out of work. Repair jobs helped pay the bills, but they weren't nearly as satisfying as remodels where a guy could feel he'd actually created something. Cleaning up other people's mistakes wasn't his idea of fun.

Standing, he holstered his claw hammer and, fighting

the wind, moved carefully toward the ladder. From here he had a clear view of other houses dotting the coast and of the Pacific beyond, frothing with whitecaps. This was what he wanted—a home overlooking the ocean. *In your dreams, buddy. The day you have a house in the six- or seven-digit range is the day a tsunami swamps the whole damn West Coast.*

Swinging over the edge of the roof, he started down the ladder, then stopped, his eyes fixed on the Greer cottage in the distance. Isolated from its neighbors, vulnerable to sun and storms, it represented the quality craftsmanship of a bygone era. He squinted. Lights shone from the windows. Was the old lady back? Odd. She hadn't been here in a long time. Parked in front of the house was an older-model car. Surely not Geneva's. She drove only flashy foreign cars. Usually red or yellow. Shrugging at his idle train of thought, he clambered to the ground.

Bubba, his half Lab, half German shepherd, jumped from the bed of Kyle's pickup and danced delighted circles around him, as if knowing they would shortly be on their way home. Kyle knelt beside the dog, scratching the thick fur behind his ears. "Hey, fella, ready for the barn?" Nonstop tail-wagging provided a clear answer. Kyle opened the door of the cab. "Hop in, buddy. But don't get too excited. We have to stop by the office on our way home."

It was nearly five-thirty when they rolled into the lot of Nemec Construction. The company vehicles were already aligned in rows, and the warehousemen were heading out the door. Clouds gathering in the west obscured the weak April sun, so Kyle tucked his sunglasses in the pocket of his denim work shirt. "Wanna come see Rita?" The dog perked up his ears and eyed Kyle expectantly. Kyle climbed out of the truck. "C'mon, then."

This was their evening ritual. Bubba wouldn't leave the cab until Kyle invited him. And every evening, Rita, the plump, friendly receptionist, had a doggie treat waiting in the office.

When they entered, Rita looked up from her computer. "Hey, handsome, who's your friend?" She winked at Kyle, as she always did. Bubba sat beside her desk, his tail wagging. "Have you been a good boy today?" The dog lifted one leg and pawed the floor, a trick she had taught him. "Okay, Bubba. Here you are." She pulled a box of dog biscuits from her drawer and gave him one. He mouthed it and scurried off to a corner to enjoy the morsel.

"You're spoiling him."

"Nonsense. He just needs some good mommy-loving." She raised an eyebrow. "Something he sure can't get from you."

Kyle laughed. "Jeez, I hope not. We're manly bachelors."

"Don't you think it's time you found a better bed partner than a hairy beast?"

"Meddling again?"

"Somebody needs to, you big blockhead."

"I suppose you've got somebody in mind?" The minute the words left his mouth, he wished them unsaid.

Rita nodded imperceptibly toward the office area behind the glass divider at her back.

Kyle followed her gaze, then shifted awkwardly from one foot to the other. Rosemary. It figured. "Wouldn't that be a cliché? Dating the boss's daughter?"

Rita tapped a pen impatiently. "Nonsense. You know darn well you're practically like one of the family already. You could at least try to make it official."

Kyle sighed. He'd had this conversation more than once and usually offered a litany of excuses. Rosemary was younger. He couldn't date the bratty little sister of his best friend. He might be accused of currying favor with the boss. She was a nice girl, but nice girls weren't his type. None of it had deterred Rita.

Nor Rosemary, who continued to flirt and look at him with hope. Rosemary, who had Pete's eyes. In a way, Kyle wished he could be attracted to her. Rita was right about one thing. It did get damn lonely in that mobile home of his. And he was sick to death of his own cooking. Even so, he was better off not encouraging Rosemary. He needed to keep his relationships with the Nemecs on as businesslike a basis as possible, to know he'd earned every responsibility Bruce Nemec had given him.

"Here." He thrust his notes into Rita's hands. "Can you write up the bid for the Brady place and mail it to them?"

"Sure." Rita tucked the paper into a folder and stood. "Got big plans for tonight? After all, it's Friday."

"I figure I'll treat myself to an evening at the Yacht Club," he said, referring to a local bar near the fishing pier.

"That'll be a novelty. Do you ever go anyplace else?"

"Nah, why change my routine?"

Rita picked up her sweater from the back of her chair and shrugged into it. "You're impossible."

"That's why you love me, right?" He threw Rita a roguish grin. "See you Monday." Then he called Bubba and they headed for the truck.

On the way home, Kyle drove slowly, pondering Rita's comments. The rut he was in, though comfortable, was also paralyzing. Bruce had made no secret of the fact he was grooming Kyle to take over Nemec Construction someday. Putting him in charge of their home repair and remodeling division, AAA Builders, was a tacit step toward that end. But the company should have been Pete's. Damned if Kyle would worm his way further into the family by marrying Rosemary. Besides, she deserved more than he could give.

He didn't want to think about any of this. Especially not about Pete. Remembering was too painful. More than anything, he missed the friendship they'd shared ever since they were happy-go-lucky kids riding their bikes all over Eden Bay.

But that was then. Kyle was far from happy-go-lucky now. He survived one day at a time. Nose to the grindstone. Minding his own business. Expecting nothing.

A fog rolling in from the ocean forced him to concentrate on driving. Beside him, Bubba licked his chops, then pressed his nose to the passenger-window glass.

A man and his dog. It was enough.

THE MORNING AFTER her arrival Annie stood at the window facing the sea, watching rivulets of water smear the panes. The rain had started late last night shortly after she'd moved all her belongings to this upstairs front bedroom, the one that had always been Geneva's.

Now, because of her weakened condition, Auntie G. stayed in the downstairs bedroom. The damp Pacific coast was a far cry from the dry desert air. No welcoming sun greeted Annie here. But what had she expected? In memory, she'd always pictured Eden Bay through a scrim of gray mist.

Pulling the oversize plaid flannel shirt closer around her, she turned to study the room. Although most of her aunt's belongings had been moved, the double bed with the inlaid wood headboard and its matching dresser were still here, as were several of Geneva's oil paintings, including the one Annie had always liked best—a rocky beach scene with white-tipped, emerald waves crashing against the shore.

A wide, six-foot-long table stood against the north wall. Annie didn't know where it had come from, but Geneva's thoughtfulness of providing a worktable made Annie feel at home in a way little else could have.

Moving to the first box, she unpacked multicolored scraps of upholstery material and stacked them beneath the table. In a second carton she located shears, scissors, spools of thread, braiding and her large button box. She arranged these items neatly on the left, then pulled a piece of cranberry floral material from the fabric pile and spread it across the surface, visualizing the exact way she wanted to cut it to transform it into a satin-lined tote. For the first time since Carmen's call, she felt the coils of tension ease.

Keeping busy was the answer. Between caring for Geneva and burying herself in work, there would be no time to think, to remember.

At the sound of a light tap on the door, she said, "Come in."

Carmen waited with a tray. "Breakfast, Annie? Your *tia*, she is still sleeping."

With the first whiff of blueberry scones and coffee, Annie realized she was ravenous. "Thank you, Carmen." She moved across the room and took the tray. "But I don't need to be waited on."

"Maybe just for today." In the woman's eyes, Annie read understanding.

Annie set down the tray. "Will you call me when Geneva is awake?"

"*Sí.* Your visit, it is bringing her joy."

"What have her doctors said?"

Carmen shook her head. "Better to ask her. It is not for me to tell."

"I need the truth."

"She is strong. She is not afraid of that truth." Carmen nodded at the tray. "If you want more, come to the kitchen."

"Thank you." Annie closed the door behind Carmen, then sat with her breakfast in a chintz-covered armchair. The scone was buttery and delicious and the coffee strong and hot. Neither, however, filled the empty place within her.

LATER THAT MORNING when Annie entered the living room, Geneva looked up and smiled. "Good morning, petunia." She gestured toward the bay window. "Nice day for ducks."

"Typical Oregon." Taking the chair across from her

aunt's, she noticed that Geneva was wearing a colorful Moroccan-style caftan. "How are you? Did you eat your breakfast?"

Geneva gave a dismissive wave of her hand. "I'd rather not dwell on my health, but I did eat a poached egg."

Annie tried to match her aunt's bantering tone. "And that's a cause for celebration?"

"Bells, whistles and firecrackers." Geneva cocked her head, studying Annie. "Did you sleep well?"

"Fine," Annie lied. No point mentioning the hours she'd lain awake listening to the wind and wishing Geneva still felt like trotting around the globe gathering information and anecdotes for her travel books.

"I don't believe you." Her aunt hesitated. "Everything must seem strange to you. The town, the cottage—" she gestured airily "—and me. No wonder. I feel strange to myself. I keep thinking I can run upstairs, walk on the beach, drive a car." She sighed. "I guess I should be thankful I'm still breathing, because we have work to do."

"Work?"

"See that chest over there by the piano? Bring it to me."

Annie pushed the heavy container across the floor to Geneva, who leaned over and, with effort, opened the lid. Inside were sheafs of paper, along with photo albums.

"This, my dear niece, is Greer family memorabilia. You are my only descendant, and I don't want our history to die with me."

Annie picked up a packet of letters tied with binding twine. "You're the only Greer I really know. I have sketchy memories of my father, but I was only five when he died. It's as if he's the star of a long-ago movie that I can scarcely remember, no matter how hard I try to rewind."

"We can't bring him back, but we can certainly flesh out some of those memories and more. If nothing else, Greers have always been unique individuals. Look at me. I've been to six continents, had lovers on three—"

"Auntie G.!"

"Don't look so shocked. Just because I never married doesn't mean I didn't have good times. But more about that later." She paused to cough wetly into a tissue. "I thought each day we might make some headway with what's in the chest. You can work in the afternoon while I rest."

"I'd like that," Annie said quietly.

"You know, this house is falling apart. The porch railings are loose and there are water spots upstairs. I don't want to even think about dry rot around the doors and windows. Would you mind going through the place to check for problem areas?"

"Not at all."

"I'll phone my neighbor Frances Gardner for recommendations for a repairman—it's been so long since I lived here. I want to get this done."

Annie recognized the steel in Geneva's voice and the implied message: *before I die.* "I'll get right on it."

"Good. Then after my nap, I'm challenging you to a game of gin rummy. Winner gets an extra glass of wine." Her eyes glinted mischievously.

"Are you even supposed to drink?"

"One glass. But that's if I lose. Which I won't."

Annie wanted to argue, to implore her aunt to do exactly what the doctor had ordered. Yet, if her days were numbered, what harm could a second glass of wine do in the big scheme of things?

The phone rang and Annie heard Carmen answer it in the kitchen. After a few moments, she appeared in the doorway, her expressive eyes filled with tears.

Geneva stretched out her hand. "Carmen, what is it, dear?"

"My daughter. She's had her baby. A *niño,* a boy. Too soon. Three months soon. I… She needs help with my granddaughter."

"Of course, you must go." Geneva's tone brooked no argument. "As soon as you can."

"But you are sick and—"

"Annie is here and she will take care of me."

Carmen wiped her eyes. "*Gracias, señorita.* I go now and pack. Annie, you come and I tell you about caring for your *tia.*"

The rest of the day passed in a blur of instructions and arrangements. At Geneva's insistence that she could be left alone, Annie drove Carmen to catch a shuttle at the nearby beach resort.

When Annie returned to the cottage in the late afternoon, she noticed there were no lights shining from the house. She found Geneva asleep in her chair, her skin ashen and her breath labored, despite the oxygen tank.

Annie panicked. What did she know about caring for a dying woman? With Carmen away, Annie would be forced into the community—to the grocery, the pharmacy, the gas station. There would be no avoiding people. People who would not welcome her presence. People who would blame her.

MONDAY MORNING Kyle dragged himself into consciousness, battling images of his recurring nightmare. Drenched in sweat, he sat on the side of the bed cradling his aching head in his hands. *Damn it, damn it, damn it!* The dream always started so innocently, luring him into the vortex of horror. The details might change, but the ending never did. Dressed in period costume, he stood on a scaffolding, holding in his hand a long-handled ax, dripping with blood. And staring up at him with a gentle but distorted smile was Pete, his head severed from his neck.

It didn't take a shrink to get the symbolism. The hell of it was, he lived it every day, with or without the dream. Each time he passed the field where he and Pete had played American Legion baseball, reported to the National Guard Armory or shook hands with Bruce.

Why couldn't it have been him? What did he have to live for compared to Pete? A mother who'd abandoned him and a father who beat the crap out of him on a regular basis? Certainly not a beautiful girl he loved with every fiber of his being. Nor a future full of promise.

Kyle shut his eyes to the photo on his dresser of him and Pete, arms around each other's shoulders, caps tilted cockily, on their last day of leave before deployment to Afghanistan.

Slowly the sensation of Bubba licking his toes pulled him from his thoughts.

After a long, hot shower and a bowl of instant oatmeal, he felt minimally better. It would be a relief to go to work. There he wouldn't have time to brood.

Rita eyed him speculatively when he arrived at the office. "You're late."

"So?"

"Just commenting because you're almost never late."

He shrugged, disinclined to engage in their usual banter.

"Well," she drawled, "maybe you're excused just this once. Besides, if you'd already been on the job, you'd have missed this." She handed him a phone memo.

"Huh? The Greer place?" He studied the message requesting an estimate on repairs. "I thought I saw a car there last week."

"Frankly, Geneva didn't sound good. Told me she wants to get her place fixed up ASAP. Before she dies, she said. Talk about a conversation stopper. I didn't know what to say to that, so I told her we'd have someone out today."

The Greer cottage had always had a special charm. He was sorry about the old lady, but he'd love to get his hands on that house.

CHAPTER TWO

THE MORNING HAD NOT gone well. Figuring out Auntie G.'s medications and dressing her had taken longer than Annie had predicted. Then she'd burned the toast and undercooked the eggs. Geneva had waved off her apology, daintily dipping a corner of her toast in the runny yolk, but beyond that, eating nothing.

After breakfast, even though she seemed tired, Geneva insisted that Annie help her into her living room chair. Managing the walker and the oxygen tank at the same time was difficult, but finally she had her aunt settled, the afghan over her knees, a book in her lap.

"I'll be fine here. Go, get the kitchen cleaned up, take a shower. Don't worry about me."

After loading the dishwasher and wiping down the counter, Annie checked on Geneva, who sat staring out the window with her open book facedown. Annie bathed quickly, worried that she wouldn't hear Geneva if she called. Or fell. Annie toweled her hair, then threw on a shapeless blue T-shirt over gray sweatpants and was slipping on her Crocs when she heard Geneva ring the bell she'd given her to use as a summons. Annie raced down the stairs. "What is it?"

"Calm down. The repairman I've been expecting is coming up the walk."

Through the bay window Annie saw a white pickup with red lettering on the door. AAA Builders Home Repair and Remodeling. "That was fast."

"I told you I wanted the cottage fixed. And I want it done properly. This company came with high recommendations." A heavy knock sounded on the door.

Running her fingers through her damp hair, Annie walked to the front hall and threw open the door.

The world fell away. She couldn't breathe, much less utter a sound. She leaned against the doorjamb, a wave of dizziness threatening her balance.

"Annie?" The blond-haired man hovered over her, his strong, broad-shouldered body blocking the sun, his chiseled facial features pale beneath his tan. Then he turned away, swiped the ball cap from his head and paced to one end of the porch and back, stopping in front of her, his gray eyes icy. "You've got some nerve showing up in Eden Bay."

Annie gripped the door, focusing on his chest, on the forest-green of his chamois shirt, on anything but those accusing eyes. If she could focus there, she could stop the memories—Pete, Kyle…her reasons for leaving town. "I…I…" She faltered, realizing there was absolutely nothing she could say to Kyle.

"Don't even try to explain." He placed the cap back on his head. "Find someone else for this job."

"Annie?" Geneva's imperious voice pierced the silence. "I want to see that young man."

Kyle hesitated.

"Look," Annie said in a low enough tone that Geneva couldn't hear, "my aunt's sick and wants this place fixed up."

"There are plenty of guys who can do it."

"You were recommended."

He peered over her head into the interior. "All right. I'll tell her no myself." He stepped around her and strode into the living room.

Struggling for equilibrium, Annie sank onto the stairs, listening to the rise and fall of voices. After Kyle told her great-aunt he would be unavailable to do the repairs, she heard Geneva's voice but couldn't make out the words. After a few minutes, Kyle returned, his expression grim. He paused in the doorway. "Have your damn list ready. I'll be here Wednesday morning." He put his hand on the doorknob, then spoke again. "One more thing. Stay out of my way." Then he was gone.

Slowly Annie released her death grip on the banister. Why had she ever thought she could hide out here? Avoid the disapproval, even hatred, of those in Eden Bay?

Her muscles tensed. She longed to leave this place. Now.

"Annie?"

She took a deep breath, then went into the living room.

Her aunt's color had improved and her face bore a triumphant smile. "Well, everything's settled. That's a very professional young man." She adjusted her nose-piece. "Did you know him when you lived here?"

Annie nodded, dreading further questioning.

"He seems nice. Maybe you should get in touch with some of your old friends."

"No."

The smile faded from Geneva's lips. "It was a long time ago, dear."

"They haven't forgotten. Or forgiven."

ADRENALINE PUMPING, Kyle gunned the truck down the driveway then onto the Coast Highway where he abruptly pulled into a scenic overlook. Oblivious to Bubba's quizzical look, he gripped the wheel, stared at the ocean and swore at the top of his lungs. Finally, with the cab closing in on him, he climbed out and gulped in sea-fresh air, haunted by what that bitch Annie had done to Pete ten years ago.

As if it were yesterday, he was in Pete's bedroom listening to his friend's voice break with emotion. "She's gone, man. Just like that. What did I do?" Pete clutched a crumpled envelope.

Kyle had thought to be supportive by telling him no girl was worth it. Wrong tactic. Pete loved Annie with an intensity that defied reason. They were the perfect couple, the ones who would be as crazy in love in their nineties as they were in their teens. That's why her abrupt departure was so twisted, made no sense.

"You don't get it, Kyle. I can't live without her. I'm going after her."

Kyle picked up the Dear John letter and scanned it. "Forget her. It says right here she wants a new life. Without you. Besides, you can't go after her. We leave for National Guard training tomorrow."

Pete howled Annie's name. Kyle wrapped him in a bear hug, while Pete said, "Something's not right. Something's not right."

The roar of the surf filled Kyle's head. A lot of some-things weren't right. Annie had no business coming back to Eden Bay and stirring up the past. Her presence would remind everyone of Pete, of his never-ending search for her—a search that bordered on desperate—of the way her disappearance had slowly drained the vitality from him.

Worse, she would remind Kyle of all the ways he'd let down his best friend and all the reasons why that sniper should have hit him, not Pete.

What a mess. And so typical of Kyle's life. The chance to work on a gem of a house like he'd always wanted tainted by seeing her every day. Every time he saw her—still beautiful, damn it, despite the lack of makeup and the too-big clothes—he could remember how close he came to betraying Pete.

Kyle sighed. The least he could do was protect the Nemecs from her. The last thing they needed was her stirring up their grief. Man, she was trouble. He had hoped never to see her again because he was afraid of what he'd say to her, do to her.

Yet when she'd opened the door this morning, his breath had stopped. A part of him was glad to see her. And that's the part of himself he damned to hell.

PROPPED UP on three bed pillows, Geneva stared at the ceiling, wide-awake. When she was younger, she'd hated such sleepless nights. Now they were a blessing.

They meant more time to remember, to plan, to *be*. She'd asked Annie to crack the window so she could hear the waves lapping the rocky beach in a soothing lullaby. And smell the tangy salt air that transported her to so many of the places she'd visited—the Greek Islands, Australia, Tahiti. It had been a good life, full of adventure and fascinating people. And no small measure of success. For most people enough satisfaction for a lifetime.

But not for her until this one last thing was done—helping Annie *live*.

Geneva rued the fact she'd been halfway around the world when Annie had needed her all those years ago. Annie had fled Eden Bay in a panic, for reasons she had never shared. Geneva had been unable to help. The best she'd been able to do from so far away was direct Annie to Nina Valdez in Bisbee, Arizona.

Geneva had first met Nina at a women's consciousness-raising retreat in Mexico where they'd struck up an enduring friendship. Nina owned a small café and herb shop, and under Nina's wing, Annie had found sanctuary, but not the happy, fulfilling life Geneva wished for her. The way Nina described it in a letter, Annie was simply doing what people expected of her. Making no waves. Forming no close friendships. Calmly and dispassionately *existing*. Annie deserved more. Needed more. Needed to live.

For a brief time this morning, Geneva had thought the appearance of Kyle might offer Annie a connection to the town. But Annie had made it perfectly clear that she wanted no part of him or anyone else she had once known.

Something continued to eat at Annie. Something that

had happened here. And until she faced it directly, she was doomed to a half-life.

Geneva closed her eyes. *Give me time, please, to help this lost girl.* Then, lulled by the wash of the ocean, she drifted to sleep.

WEDNESDAY MORNING Kyle parked his pickup beside Annie's well-used Honda, wishing he had not let the old lady get to him. She had skillfully used both flattery and her failing health as inducements for him to take on this work. Ever since, he'd been cursing his gullibility and stupidity. He did not need this job. He did not want this job. And, especially, he did not want to be on the same planet with Annie Greer, much less in the same house.

He let Bubba out for a brief run, then had him hop into the truck bed. "Stay. Be a good boy, fella. Stay." As if sensing the undercurrent in his master's voice, Bubba's ears perked up. "Yeah, I know. I'm not the happiest camper." Kyle grinned wryly, then picked up his tool chest and plodded toward the cottage, noting, without conscious effort, the loose guttering on the ocean side. Hopefully there wouldn't be that much on the repair list. But the sagging front door, the weatherworn shingles and the loose shutters were not good omens. He set down the chest, took a deep breath and rapped on the door.

When Annie answered his knock, she stood aside and directed him to the living room. He nodded coolly, then brushed past her. Geneva sat before the bay window. Two chairs faced her and on the table between them was a typed list. Without a word, Annie indicated he should take the chair closer to the window. Then she perched on the other, as if poised for a quick getaway.

To Kyle's relief, Geneva broke the tension. "Well, young man, I'm delighted you're here. My niece has gone over the house thoroughly and prepared a list."

As he read, the silence was broken only by the melodic tinkling of an outdoor wind chime and Geneva Greer's oxygen tank. Beside him, Annie sat primly, back straight, fingers laced, jaw rigid. Yeah, well, she wasn't the only one who didn't want to be here.

Still, the house lured him. He took in the crafted mantel and staircase, the patina of the hardwood floors, the high ceilings, the beveled glass in the built-in breakfront. This house was a woodworker's paradise.

"Well?" Geneva studied him with alert blue eyes.

"It looks like a complete list, although I'll have to inspect everything myself."

"I would expect that. I'm prepared to pay well for you to complete this job quickly. As you know—" she paused, as if summoning strength "—I have little time left to enjoy your handiwork. And it is *your* handiwork I want."

He heard Annie's quick intake of breath, but still she said nothing.

"I'll have to leave occasionally to check on my men. Yours isn't the only project we've got going."

"Understandable, but I want the best, so I'd prefer that you do the bulk of the work."

"I'll try." He rose to his feet, wondering if he'd lost his senses. "Perhaps Annie will give me a tour and point out what needs to be done."

When Annie stood, a fragrance like summer roses engulfed him, taking him back to senior prom and the two dances he'd had with her. The two dances Pete had grudgingly relinquished to him. And if Pete had known what was going through Kyle's head, he would have never let Annie within ten miles of him.

"We'll start outside," she said, as she led the way to the front door.

OUT ON THE PORCH, her turtleneck sweater offering little protection against the raw wind, Annie wanted to push Kyle away, avoid the man who represented her demons. She wanted to scream at the top of her lungs, somehow release the panic welling in her. Yet her loyalty to Geneva took precedence. "This is on the list," she said, indicating the rickety porch railing.

Hugging herself against the chill, she waited while he tested each post. When he finished, she walked around the side of the house and pointed at the guttering.

"I saw that earlier," he said.

She was grateful when the tour continued in this manner: him carefully appraising each flaw, her accommodating him only so far as was necessary. When they came to her bedroom, though, she stopped in the doorway, blocking his entry. She didn't want him in her space, violating her privacy. Just thinking of his having personal knowledge of her worktable, her bed, her toiletries laid out on the dresser made her feel exposed.

He came up beside her, crowding her with his hard, toned body. "Excuse me," he said, "but isn't this where the ceiling leak is?"

More in an effort to get away from him than to allow him entrance, she stepped away. He strode into the room, dwarfing the dainty rocker by the door. She pointed to the northwest corner. "Over there."

As he studied the telltale signs of water damage, she watched for any change in his expression. Any time now he would ask her the question hanging between them: *Why did you treat Pete so heartlessly?*

FOR DINNER THAT EVENING Kyle fixed a frozen pizza, then grabbed a bottle of beer and settled on his dilapidated couch to watch the Mariners game. Bubba, quite a pepperoni fan, made a pass at his plate. "No way, buddy. You had your supper. Alpo. Yummy."

Bubba gave up and settled, head on his paws, under the small kitchen table.

Kyle took a swig of beer and fixed his gaze on the screen. Bottom of the seventh inning. Two outs, two men on base. He let his mind wander to the upcoming weekend. Friday night's company softball game. Then the party at the Nemecs' to celebrate Rosemary's birthday. His Saturday fishing date with Buzz Royer, the company electrician.

Then, diabolically, his thoughts turned to Annie. Her aloof behavior. The way she'd looked at him in her bedroom, as if he were an intruder bent on no good. Her whole snow-queen routine would get old. Because the hell of it was he was going to be spending considerably more time than he liked at the Greer cottage, which had been neglected too long and needed a great deal of work. He didn't appreciate her treating him like the bad guy. He wasn't the one who'd run away. He wasn't the one who'd devastated Pete. Sure, Kyle had his own sins to atone for, but he'd stuck by Pete to the end.

Still, one thing was for damn sure. Before Kyle finished with the house, he'd get some answers from her. She owed him. More important, she owed Pete and the Nemecs.

He tossed back the rest of the beer, then glanced at the TV. Bottom of the eighth? Hell, he'd missed more than half an inning. He swung to his feet and snagged a second brew from the fridge. *Enough about Annie,* he told himself. *You don't need this aggravation in your life.* Tomorrow, weather permitting, he was working outside. He would concentrate on the job. Put her out of his mind. Exactly where she belonged. Where she always should have belonged.

AFTER SUPPER Annie undertook the task she'd been putting off—making an inventory of food supplies. Although Carmen had left a well-stocked pantry and some frozen casseroles, Annie would have to make a trip to the supermarket, even if a raging case of cabin fever was preferable. For a change of scene and to work off tension, she'd been walking on the beach each afternoon while Geneva napped.

Annie was compiling a grocery list when the phone rang. The warmth of Nina Valdez's voice was a balm. "Your friends are missing you. So am I. And the customers? They're always asking after you."

Annie doubted she had left such a void in the lives of Bisbee residents. Maybe in Nina's, though. "I miss everyone. I wish I were there."

"How is she, honey?" Nina's voice registered concern.

"I'm not really sure." As she talked, Annie carried the phone onto the front porch and curled up in the swing. "She isn't giving me all the details and for now, she's holding her own. But I can see it's a struggle for her, and one day she'll have to give in."

"Do you have help?"

An onslaught of loneliness blindsided her. "Mmm, not really. Not now. But Carmen will be back soon."

"Have you considered hospice care?"

Nina might as well have socked her in the stomach. *Hospice.* The word floated in her awareness like a circling vulture.

"Annie?"

"I'm here," she whispered.

"I didn't mean to upset you. But I don't want you facing this on your own."

"She's really dying, isn't she?" Annie had known that intellectually, but she'd avoided saying it aloud. Somehow verbalizing made it real.

"Yes, honey, she is. You know that's why I encouraged you to go home to Oregon."

Tears rolled down Annie's cheeks. "She's…she's…" Her voice caught. "My family." *My only family* was left unsaid.

From that point, she couldn't focus on the conversation, but she did hear the empathy and love in Nina's voice.

After Annie hung up, she stayed on the porch to pull herself together. Then she went into the living room, where she and Geneva played two games of gin rummy. At nine, after a fit of coughing, Geneva declared she was ready for bed. Annie helped her undress. When Geneva was finally tucked in for the night, she reached up and grabbed Annie's hand. "Thank you for making the list for Kyle Becker. I can't wait to see how the renovation turns out."

Hearing the delight in her aunt's voice, Annie realized this house project had given Geneva a purpose. But when it was completed...?

As she gently squeezed her aunt's hand and leaned over to kiss her, she wished she could ask Kyle to take all the time in the world to finish his work.

Oddly, when she was finally in her own bedroom, it seemed as if the man himself were there. His scent lingered in the air and the memory of his presence made her pulse race. She found herself remembering the fun-loving eighteen-year-old jock who had been Pete's best friend. Her friend, too, teasing her unmercifully about her studious ways, about the glints of red in her hair, and, of course, about how gaga she was over Pete. Most of the time Kyle had been full of laughter and jokes, but every now and then she had sensed that beneath his cheerful facade lay a serious side, even a vulnerable one, possibly a result of his troubled home life.

Today she'd seen only the serious Kyle. It was the hurt she saw. Unexpectedly, that made her feel sad—and guilty. Pete's death clearly haunted them both.

CHAPTER THREE

By FRIDAY AFTERNOON Kyle and Annie had settled into
a kind of compromise. So long as he worked outside,
she stayed inside. The two times he'd had to work in the
house, Annie had pulled on a shapeless gray crewneck
sweater and headed for the beach. They only communicated when necessary.

By contrast, the more he was around Geneva, the
greater his respect for her. So few home owners really
knew what they wanted, and he often spent as much
time undoing their decisions as he did on the actual
work. No such problem with Geneva. Insofar as was
possible, she wanted the house restored to its original
splendor, and she knew exactly what that would look
like. Best of all, she was willing to pay.

This morning she had shown him photos of the
exterior, circa 1936. Built to withstand the coastal
weather, the cottage was functional yet beautiful in its
New England simplicity. The design had been lovingly
executed, and Kyle wanted it to be lovingly preserved.
Some jobs were merely that—jobs. The rare few, like
this one, stirred something deep in his soul.

As he was leaving for the day, he met Annie returning from the beach. He couldn't just ignore her, but what came out of his mouth was sarcastic. "Got big plans for the weekend?"

She looked straight through him. "I'm not here for fun," she said, and continued to the house.

No, in a real sense, she wasn't here for fun. But the way she frowned and kept to herself suggested she didn't know much about fun anymore. Not that it was any of his business.

Bubba gave a short bark of greeting, happy to run around for a few minutes before hopping into the cab. Kyle watched him, but his thoughts were on his senior year in high school. They'd all had fun then. Pete the quarterback, him the running back. Annie, in her short-skirted cheerleading outfit, her shining hair caught up in a big blue bow. Postgame parties on the beach, sparks from a bonfire spiraling into the starry sky, beer flowing freely. Sometimes Pete brought his guitar and, accompanied by the rat-a-tat of makeshift driftwood bongos and the cadence of the surf, they would all sing along until gradually, one by one, the couples slipped off into the darkness.

Almost as a self-protective device, he realized now, he'd cultivated a devil-may-care, bad-boy image, and there had been no shortage of willing girls climbing all over him. But none of them had been Annie.

A burning sensation filled Kyle's throat. He fought the disturbing images.

And what about his own weekends these days? Compared to Annie, he had only minimal bragging rights. How many alcohol-buzzed evenings could a person spend at the Yacht Club playing pool and flirting with the barmaids? Or, big deal, watching ESPN until his eyes glazed over?

At least tonight he had the softball game to look forward to. That was the good news. The bad news? Rosemary's birthday party, where subtly and not so subtly the matchmakers would be zeroing in on him.

"Bubba, I swear to God, I'm gonna die a bachelor."

ANNIE PULLED a deck of cards from the pocket of her overalls and sat down across from her aunt. "Gin rummy tonight, Auntie G.?"

"No, petunia. I want to start on the family history." From the chest, which had remained by her chair, she reached for a stack of photographs. "We'll begin with my father and mother." She drew out a picture of a handsome, dark-haired young man, wearing a World War I uniform and looking directly into the camera. "This is my father. He went over to France with the first wave of Yanks. In all the years I knew him, he never once talked about his war experiences. Only about the fine friends he'd made, many lost in the trenches." She paused, thinking of all those soldiers who never returned home. "One of those friends gave my father a wonderful piece of advice in early 1929. 'Sell your stock,' he said. Because of my father's respect for the man, he did exactly that, only a few short months before the October crash."

"I've always wondered how he managed to build this house during the Depression." Annie fingered the faded photograph. "What about your mother?"

"Lucy Windsor was from a wealthy Connecticut

family that summered in Maine. Shortly after the war, she fell madly in love with William Greer and, despite her parents' objections that he didn't come from the 'proper' stock, she defied them by marrying him and, in essence, living happily ever after."

The ghost of a smile teased Annie's lips. "I'm beginning to see where your independent streak may have originated."

"You come from a strong line, my dear." Geneva pointed to a photo of a blond beauty with bobbed hair, clad in a fringed flapper-style evening gown. "My mother. People always loved being around her. My father built the cottage for her. She longed for the sea of her childhood, and he gave her the next best thing. Even though we lived in Portland, we spent every summer here. Happy times."

"I've always thought this house had ghosts, the good kind."

Geneva nodded. "That's why it's so important to me to preserve this place."

In her great-aunt's words Annie heard the plaintive melody of nostalgia. "I hope new owners love and honor the cottage the way you do."

"New owners? I'm not fixing up the house to sell it." Geneva smiled, then picked up Annie's hand and held it in her own. "Oh, my little petunia, this place will be yours."

Annie's mind reeled. Hers? That would mean staying in Eden Bay. "Auntie G., I'm not sure—"

"This is your home. In time, I pray you will come to embrace this place."

What could she possibly say to her great-aunt? The

gift of the cottage was more than generous. How could she disappoint Auntie G. by telling her she had no desire to remain in a town with such distressing memories? "I can't promise anything."

The older woman nodded in understanding. "Not now, maybe. Just promise me you'll give Eden Bay a chance."

It was a lot to ask, but under the circumstances she had little choice but to murmur, "I'll try."

Later, as Annie snuggled under the comforter that smelled vaguely of lavender, she pondered how different things might have been for her in Eden Bay, if only… She shuddered and drew the spread up over her shoulders. So much had changed, and her future was a huge question mark. In another world, she might have been the one to continue the line of Greers living in the cottage. Now they would die out with Geneva.

Perhaps that was just as well.

BY THE TIME Kyle raced home from the softball game, showered, changed and drove to the Nemecs' house, the party was in full swing, the celebration enhanced by the Nemec Construction Tigers' 10-3 win. "The conquering hero arrives," trumpeted Wade Hanson, the finish carpenter. The men clustered around a beer keg looked up and cheered. "Great pitching, Becker," one of them said.

"You guys weren't too shabby yourselves. Fifteen hits, no errors. You know what?" He grinned and ambled toward the keg. "I think we all deserve a beer." Somebody thrust one into his hand. He made quick work of it and refilled the cup. It was a clear, cool night, and if he had a choice, he'd stay out here talking about the upcoming NBA playoffs and shooting the breeze with the fellas. He pictured the women gathered in the family room, undoubtedly talking about kids and recipes and stuff. Times like this, he was glad he wasn't married.

As if that thought had summoned her, Wade's wife, Carrie, appeared, hooked her arm through Kyle's and started toward the house. "Come on in, you guys. It's time for the cake."

With Kyle in tow, Carrie walked through the kitchen, past the dining room table laden with assorted appetizers and into the family room. "Here he is," she called to the assembled throng, as if she'd just reeled in a prize salmon. "The winning pitcher."

Bruce Nemec sidled up behind him and whispered, "Into the frying pan, son."

The women cooed their congratulations. One stood outside the circle, smiling, never taking her eyes off him. Rosemary. "Sit down," Bruce's wife, Janet, urged. "There. Next to the birthday girl."

Kyle complied, even throwing in a gentlemanly kiss on the cheek. "Happy birthday, Rosemary."

"It is now," she said, lowering her voice and laying a hand on his knee.

Someone dimmed the lights and Pete and Rosemary's older sister, Margaret, entered the room, bearing a sheet cake with lit candles. The crowd began singing "Happy Birthday," and when Margaret set the cake on a table, Kyle could finally read the message written in frosting. *This is the year! Happy twenty-fifth!*

The year for what? The girl had only one goal, one dream—marriage. Just then somebody had the nerve to call out, "Make a wish, Rosie."

And damned if she didn't blow out every one of those twenty-five candles.

While everyone was eating, Kyle excused himself and escaped down the hall toward the bedrooms and guest bath. The door to Pete's old room, normally closed, stood open. Against his instincts, Kyle went inside, shutting the door behind him. He turned on the table lamp and stood in the middle of the room, trying to recall what it had looked like when he and Pete had spent hours sprawled on the floor with their Hot Wheels track or sitting at the desk playing Tetris on Pete's computer. The army reserve recruiting poster was gone, as were those of assorted athletes and rock stars. The walls had been painted a dove-gray, and the NASCAR curtains had been replaced with something floral. Kyle closed his eyes, summoning the essence of Pete. Nothing. Finally he moved to turn off the lamp.

There—carved in the wooden surface of the table— were the initials PN and KB with the date—6/6/90. They had just finished fifth grade. Kyle remembered the day vividly. His father had come home drunk from the job at the fish cannery. In memory, Kyle could still smell his rank body and sour-sweet bourbon breath. Joe Becker had taken one look at the sink full of dirty dishes and turned on Kyle. "You worthless piece of shit," he'd shouted as he slammed him into the wall of their shoddy trailer house. Over and over. Eventually Kyle had escaped and run as fast as he could to the Nemec home.

He'd rapped on Pete's bedroom window. Pete had come out into the yard and led Kyle silently down the hall and into the bedroom. This bedroom. Pete had left long enough to get an ice bag, some towels and analgesic. No medic ever treated anyone more tenderly.

Kyle studied the surface of the desk, then ran his finger over the carved indentations. It was that night they had become blood brothers, vowing to cover each other's backs. The evidence lay in the paired initials staring up at him.

Sinking onto the bed, Kyle held his head in his hands, gritting his teeth against the howl that threatened to explode from his chest. *One of us failed.*

"Son, you all right?" Bruce stood in the doorway, frowning with concern. *Son.* From early on, Mr. Nemec had called him that. The word used to flow over him like warm honey, causing him to feel special, as if he belonged. Making him believe, at least for a pocket of time, that the ratty trailer house and the brute who lived there didn't exist. But now the true son was dead, and Kyle was no substitute, no matter how warmly the Nemecs drew him into their lives. No matter how hard he wished he could fill the empty place where Pete should've been.

Raising his head, Kyle wondered what he could say. The truth was too painful. "I just needed a moment."

"With Pete." It was not a question.

"Yeah." He shrugged. "There are times I still can't accept the fact he's gone."

"I know what you mean." Bruce strolled about the

room, tracing the same path Kyle had taken earlier. "For a while, you know, we kept this room just as it was. If Janet had her way, it would have remained a shrine. But that wasn't healthy. We had to move on." He stopped in front of Kyle and put a hand on his shoulder. "It's been a long time. You need to move on, too."

Kyle wondered if he ever could, living in this town, working as Bruce's heir apparent, being embraced by the Nemecs in every possible way. Maybe he should bite the bullet and extricate himself from them. If he stayed in Eden Bay, what would be his role? How much did he owe this family who had accepted him as one of their own since he'd been a terrified little boy?

"I think Rosemary's wondering where you are."

There was his answer. He knew they were generous people who would understand if he couldn't love their daughter, but shouldn't he at least try? Yet if he did and things didn't work out between him and Rosemary, he would have knowingly hurt another Nemec.

He rose to his feet. "Sorry. I didn't mean to put a damper on the party."

Bruce clamped an arm around his shoulder as they walked down the hall. "You didn't, son."

Afterward, Kyle couldn't remember what had snapped within him. He only knew he had been helpless to control what he said next, as if the impulse had been building in him all week. "Bruce," he said, and stopped at the end of the hall. "There's something I need to tell you. It, uh, it's not easy." Then he uttered the words that removed any trace of celebration from the man's face: "Annie Greer is back in town."

ANNIE ROSE early Sunday morning, her nerves jangling. Today was the day. No longer could she put off the trip to town. They needed both groceries and medicine. So long as she had been sequestered at the cottage, she felt safe, as if nobody could see her through the fog that obscured sections of the coastline. Today, however, the skies were a brilliant blue. There wasn't a cloud to be seen, and bright sunlight glared off the beach sand. She could hide no longer.

After breakfast she helped Geneva to her chair. Annie had arranged for Frances to come while she was gone, but left her cell number on the pad on the table and made sure the phone was at her great-aunt's elbow. "You're sure you'll be all right?"

Geneva huffed. "Frances and I will be fine. What about you?"

Annie chose to misunderstand the implication of her aunt's pointed question. "I'll be back in a jiff." That, at least, was the truth. She'd strategized that Sunday morning would be the best time for this ordeal. People would be sleeping in, at church or maybe golfing. She could dart in and out of the store, unrecognized. Anonymous.

She drew the baggy University of Arizona sweat-shirt she'd bought at a flea market over her overalls, covered her hair with a ball cap and put on her sunglasses. Maybe she'd look like a tourist. Certainly not like Annie Greer, Homecoming Queen.

To her relief, the supermarket was nearly deserted. A bored clerk stood at Register Two, and a pimply faced teen was replacing the baggies in produce. A couple of perplexed-looking men in sweats stood in front of the coffee display, and one elderly lady was picking each and every egg out of a carton, checking for cracks.

Annie grabbed a cart and made her way tentatively up and down the unfamiliar aisles. This store had not been here when she'd lived here, but it was the closest to the cottage. As a few more customers entered and the market grew more crowded, Annie felt the keen edge of panic. She had to get out of the place. She grabbed the last few items off the shelves, and it was only when she got to the checkout stand that she realized she'd selected the wrong brands of several things.

"Paper or plastic?"

She couldn't think. Finally, she blurted, "Paper."

By the time she paid and started for the car, her knees had turned to rubber. She had escaped. She imagined a comic-book bubble of dialogue floating above her head: "The invisible woman triumphs again!"

In the car, she turned on the radio and headed down the street toward the ocean and home. A radio evangelist's voice filled the air. Annie twisted the dial again. This time it was gospel music. Granted, it was Sunday morning, but surely some station was playing pop or jazz. So intent was she on tuning the radio that she nearly rear-ended the last car in a long line of vehicles stopped at the Coast Highway light. Two highway patrol cars blocked the intersection. There must've been an accident. Traffic was being diverted. Northbound to the right onto a side street; southbound to the left. Annie inched along until she made it to the side street, which wound through a brand-new subdivision. Still fiddling with the tuner and paying scant attention to her whereabouts, she followed the line of detouring cars as it entered a more established neighborhood.

Maybe it wasn't about the tuner at all. Maybe she'd been subconsciously trying to block out her surroundings. But when the line of vehicles—including her Honda—made the next turn, she saw the large hacienda-style house in the middle of the block—33 Kittiwake Road. With trembling hands she managed to pull over to the curb and open the car door before vomiting into the street, her vision blurred by tears.

HANDS FOLDED in her lap, Geneva sat quietly, waiting, worrying. She'd always tried to be a positive person. If only she could be positive about Annie and her future. Isolating herself here indefinitely was unhealthy. If Annie didn't open up soon about what was worrying her, Geneva would have no choice but to force the conversation.

She remembered that morning after high school graduation when Annie had called her at the hotel in Bangkok and told her she had to get away. She'd begged her great-aunt to help her. When Geneva had pressed Annie for details, the girl had refused to say anything more. Yet there'd been no mistaking the panic in her voice. Reluctantly, Geneva had given Annie instructions, called her friend Nina and wired money to Bisbee.

From that time to this, despite Geneva's frequent probing, Annie had never spoken about any of her friends, about her mother and George Palmer, her stepfather, or about why she had needed to flee Eden Bay.

Geneva shuddered to think what hideousness lay beneath her niece's refusal to talk.

She brooded, unaware of the passage of time. When the
front door opened, she started. "I'm back," Annie called.

After putting away the groceries, Annie came into the
living room. Her pallor highlighted the faint freckles
running across the bridge of her nose and under her
reddened eyes. "I think I'll lie down," she said. "Something must've disagreed with me. I'm a bit queasy. Can
I get you anything before I go?"

What Geneva said aloud was "No." What she was
thinking was *Child, you can get me the truth.*

ANNIE BURROWED into the folds of the downy comforter,
overwhelmed by a storm of long-buried emotions. She
had thought never to see 33 Kittiwake again, her happy
home for six years. The summer before her seventh-
grade year her mother had married George Palmer,
president of the local bank. Before that, she and her
mother had lived in a cramped bungalow near down-
town where Liz Greer owned a gift shop. They had
struggled on occasion, but even when times were good,
her mother had never seemed satisfied. When she started
dating George, all she could talk about was his country
club membership, the fancy dining establishments
where they ate and his elegant home in one of the best
neighborhoods.

When George had proposed, Annie remembered
feeling happy about having a new dad and the prospect
of a beautiful room with a canopy bed, a horse of her
own and all the clothes any girl could desire. Instinc-

tively she had warmed to George's smile, his fatherly hugs and the way he called her "sweetie." On their wedding day, Annie stood proudly by her ecstatic mother. She had never seen Liz Greer so happy. Holding a bouquet redolent with the scent of lilies and listening to her mother promise to love, honor and obey, Annie finally believed in fairy-tale endings.

Whatever George wanted, her mother gladly supplied. Both Liz and George expected Annie to behave in a way that reflected favorably their standing in the community. However, no matter how hard she tried to live up to their expectations, there was always the lingering suspicion that she never quite satisfied them. Even so, she'd reveled in the affection George showered upon her.

Gradually, though, she began to see that her mother's attention was almost totally fixed on George. He, on the other hand, doted on Annie and seemed more a parent than her own mother. Over time Annie began to question her mother's love, and a hole opened in her heart, ever widening, until Pete came along.

She muffled her sob. It was too painful to remember him and his gentleness, his devotion. And to remember what she'd had to do to him. To herself.

Auntie G. had sent her Pete's obituary. For two weeks she never left Nina's house, paralyzed by grief and memory. Pete represented the only time in her life when she had known the meaning of love and the sacrifices it required. Auntie G. and Nina could talk all they wanted about "moving on," but the truth was that when she abandoned Pete, she lost any chance of knowing enduring love.

Now Pete had been dead six years. Two years ago George had died of a heart attack. She had thought she'd escaped Eden Bay forever. Rolling over on her back, she stared at the ceiling, the water stain resembling a cracked heart.

Suddenly the room seemed suffocating. If she stayed here, images from the past would loom and her stomach might again revolt. Leaping up, she pulled on her old Nikes, grabbed a sweater and bolted down the stairs. Geneva assured her she would be fine if Annie left for a while.

She jogged down the drive toward the ocean. Breakers were rolling in, crashing against rocks, spilling on the sandy beach. The sun sparkled on the whitecaps, turning the foam to spun sugar. It was a beautiful day, she kept telling herself. She had to live in the moment. Anything else was too painful.

She stood for several minutes at the edge of the sea, letting its roar and rhythm soothe her. As she caught her breath and her heart rate slowed, she made up her mind. She was here. In Eden Bay. It was unreasonable to suppose she could hide indefinitely. She was an adult. It was time to begin acting like one.

Feeling better, she started off at a brisk walk, following the curve of the shore. Lost in her thoughts, she didn't see the figure walking toward her, until the person said, in a shocked tone, "Annie? Annie Greer?"

The woman's face was obscured by a broad-brimmed straw hat and sunglasses. But Annie knew the voice, and her heart plummeted. "Margaret?"

Slowly Pete's older sister removed her sunglasses and

then stood blocking Annie's way. "My father told me you were back in town. I'm sorry about your aunt, but I hope to God you're not staying long. You are not welcome in Eden Bay, not now, not ever." She stepped around Annie, put on her sunglasses and strode off down the beach.

Annie remained glued to the spot, the words "not now, not ever" echoing above the thundering surf.

CHAPTER FOUR

MARGARET'S WORDS didn't surprise Annie, but that
didn't make them any less hurtful. Walking back to the
cottage, she reminded herself of her resolution. She
wasn't about to let the disapproval of other people inter-
fere with her reason for being in Eden Bay. She was here
to care for Geneva, and that was exactly what she was
going to do.

Not that she could blame Margaret. Annie had never
wanted to hurt Pete. But on that long-ago night and in the
painful morning hours that followed, she'd had no
choice. Giving up the dreams she and Pete had shared had
taken every ounce of her strength and had left her hollow.

Auntie G. was right. She needed to face her demons.
Yet the immediacy of her revulsion when she'd seen the
Kittiwake house had scared her. She didn't want to revisit
the past, even as a means of healing. In Bisbee she had
avoided the issue; here, it confronted her everywhere.

When she reached the cottage, Geneva was dozing
in her chair, her veined hands resting on a stack of photographs in her lap. In repose, the crepelike skin on her
face sagged and she looked every one of her eighty
years. Her chest worked to pull in air, and with each ex-

halation, a ragged sigh escaped her lips. Annie smoothed back the wisps of hair on her forehead, and then went into the kitchen to make a fruit salad and warm some soup for supper.

"Annie?"

"I'm in the kitchen." She lowered the heat on the stove and went into the living room.

"I must've dropped off. Did you have a nice walk?"

Erasing the image of Margaret's stony face, Annie nodded.

"Could we eat in here on trays?"

"No problem."

"After supper I want to give you more of the family history and it's just easier to stay here to eat."

The truth, but not the whole truth, Annie suspected. Each day, in increasingly obvious ways, her great-aunt was failing.

Famished from skipping lunch and walking on the beach, Annie wolfed down her supper. Geneva, on the other hand, moved fruit around on her plate before finally spearing a chunk of pineapple and eating it. She did better with the soup, but still left half a bowl untouched. "I'm finished," she said, dabbing her lips with her napkin.

"Auntie G., you need to keep your strength up."

"I'm trying. But who are we fooling? I'm not going to live forever."

Annie seized the opening. "What have your doctors said?"

Geneva gazed directly into Annie's eyes. "That I'm terminal. Complications from my weak lungs and congestive heart failure will ultimately make breathing nearly impossible and affect other systems." She handed her tray to Annie. "That's why we have to make the most of the time I have. Starting with tonight."

In the kitchen, blinking back tears, Annie rinsed the dishes and quickly loaded them in the dishwasher. Nina had tried to warn her and she'd understood the seriousness of Geneva's situation, but hearing the word *terminal* from her great-aunt made the prospect unavoidably real.

"Do you remember your grandfather at all?" Geneva asked when they were settled in the living room.

"I saw him only a few times. When Daddy died, he came to the funeral. He brought me a doll. But I never played with it. It reminded me too much of the day of the funeral and the way the house smelled sickeningly of flowers and macaroni and cheese." Annie recalled looking up at her tall, slender grandfather with his gray hair and sad blue eyes. The man who had come not just to comfort her with a doll, but to bury his son.

Geneva stared into space before continuing. "When Caleb was born, I thought he'd been created solely for my entertainment. I was four and, from the beginning, mothered him. Summers here at the ocean were magical. I loved holding his little hand and leading him down to the beach for family picnics. As he grew older, he was a natural athlete who shared my zest for adventure. One day just before World War II we hiked so far down the beach we didn't get home until nearly dark. Our mother was frantic." She smiled at the memory, then was quiet for a moment, the hiss of the oxygen a reminder of how far removed she was from that time when she and her brother had romped at the shore.

She shuffled through the photographs, handing Annie one of a skinny young man in a swimsuit balancing on a rock, waves crashing around him, a delighted grin on his face. "He was such fun. He had a talent for friendships and a wicked sense of humor."

"What about my grandmother?"

"Jody? Like Caleb, she thrived on seeing new places, trying new things. They were married in 1951 just after they graduated from college." She sorted through the pictures until she found one of her brother in a white dinner jacket gazing adoringly at a dark-haired young woman with short, curly hair and a pixie-like grin. "Here they are. During the Korean War, Caleb joined the Marines. While he was overseas, Jody lived here in the cottage."

"I never knew that." Annie tried to picture the young woman living here alone, isolated, worrying about her husband.

"Practically the minute Caleb returned home, Jody got pregnant and nine months later, along came your father. Shortly after John's birth, Caleb was hired by a New York City bank and they moved."

"That explains why they didn't often get to Oregon."

"One reason."

Something in Auntie G.'s tone grabbed Annie's attention. "Another reason?"

"You may as well know. Caleb and Jody didn't care much for your mother. They found her attractive enough, but, well, somewhat superficial. Not well suited to John."

Annie wished she could defend her mother, instead of acknowledging the fairness of the judgment. "What about Daddy? Did he love her?"

"Yes, I think so. He did everything he could to please Liz."

Annie knew the outcome before she voiced it. "But it was never enough for her, right?"

"Oh, child, what are we doing probing into the long-ago relationships of other people? Marriages are what they are." She paused, then sighed. "I'm so tired. Please help me to bed."

Annie assisted her great-aunt to her feet and followed close behind with the oxygen tank as Geneva slowly made her way to the downstairs bedroom.

Once she had helped her into bed, Annie sat for a long time in the silence of the living room, poring over the photographs of her family—the family that now consisted only of her beloved Auntie G. and herself. She knew it was a matter of a few short weeks until that family would be reduced to one. Loneliness—so acute it was physically painful—washed over her.

KYLE FINALLY GAVE UP trying to sleep. He'd been tossing and turning since four in the morning, the sheets a tangle around his legs, his pillow lumpy and warm. Bubba's snores added to his insomnia. He'd had the nightmare again. The one about Pete. Damn Annie, anyway. Seeing her had been like picking at a scab and reopening a wound.

He sat on the edge of the bed holding his head in his hands, once again picturing Pete pausing that fatal few seconds to look at Annie's photo. Why couldn't Pete have moved on? Forgotten the high school sweetheart who'd punted him without an explanation? But no. Pete had carried the torch up to the instant he was killed. Oh, sure, after they'd finished Guard training, Pete had tried to find Annie. He'd talked to everyone who'd ever known her, interviewed the bus station agent and pored over cab company records. But he'd gotten nowhere. Her stepfather, George Palmer, was as clueless as Pete. And since Geneva Greer had not been living in Eden Bay at that time, Pete had no idea how to contact her. It was as if Annie had dropped off the face of the earth. But Pete never gave up. He lived as if he expected Annie to turn up on his doorstep any day. And the hell of it was, Pete would have welcomed her, no questions asked.

Kyle lurched to his feet. What in blue blazes was the matter with the woman? Seeing her here in Eden Bay infuriated him. Why had she waited so long to return? Crap, now he had to consider what to do about the damned letter.

Stumbling into the kitchen, he made coffee and turned to see Bubba standing in the bedroom doorway yawning. "Yeah, I know. Too early. Sorry, buddy." When he went outside to retrieve the morning paper, clouds scudded across the sky and a cool breeze ruffled the scraggly bushes in front of the mobile home. Kyle drew a deep breath before going back in. Bubba lay on the floor eyeing him curiously. Kyle shrugged. "Hell if I know why I can't sleep, fella."

When the coffee was done, he poured a cup and settled on the sofa to read the Sunday ball scores. But he couldn't concentrate.

He kept replaying Margaret's voice on the phone last night: "Kyle, what are you thinking working for the Greers? How dare Annie Greer show her face in this town! It would've been bad enough while Pete was alive, but now…? So help me God, I'll never know why my brother couldn't get over her."

And he kept seeing Annie's face, her tortured hazel eyes dominating her pale, freckled skin, her auburn hair blowing in the wind. There was something hauntingly lovely about her.

"Damn!" He threw down the paper and raked both hands through his hair. "We're going for a run, Bubba."

It was still dark when the two started down the road for the beach. Kyle pumped his arms rhythmically, punching the air in front of him. He picked up the pace, his breath coming in tortured gasps. And all the while, with the regularity of his heartbeat, came one word over and over. *Annie, Annie.*

What in the name of everlovin' God was that about? He didn't need a replay of high school angst.

LATER THAT MORNING, Kyle picked up the clipboard in his office and scanned the jobs in progress. He needed to check on the Swenson deck remodel and be at the Whites' when the crew knocked out the kitchen wall. "Rita, I'll be making the rounds today. You can catch me on my cell."

"Not going to the Greer cottage?" Her voice was studiously neutral, but the cocked eyebrow gave her away.

"I'm sending Vince. Weather forecast looks good. He can repaint the front porch." Geneva Greer surely wouldn't expect him to handle that part of the job.

"Have a good one, then."

He and Bubba headed for the truck. He fully intended to have a "good one." Being as far away from Annie as possible assured it.

The day went fast. He'd made a few suggestions to his man working on the Swensons' deck and then headed for the Stevenson project. Damn good thing. The boys had encountered a few problems and his being on the scene meant they'd had no delay in overcoming them. Time was, after all, money, as Bruce Nemec frequently reminded his employees.

Driving along the coast to pick up supplies from the lumberyard, he thought back to Friday night. He was going to have to do something about Rosemary. How did a guy say "Sorry, not interested" without hurting her and jeopardizing his relationship with her family? Somewhere out there was a guy who would adore her. But Kyle wasn't that man and he needed to deal with the issue. Sooner rather than later.

Perversely, with every mile he drove up the highway, his mind turned to what was going on at the Greer cottage. He pounded the steering wheel. Yes, that was exactly why he needed to put some distance between him and Annie. Every time he saw her he wanted to shake her and demand an explanation for what she'd done to Pete. But at the same time, damn it, he wanted to hold her and soothe away the worry lines etched in her face.

He didn't like this. Not one bit. He'd always thought of himself as an uncomplicated man. A relatively contented one.

And then *she* had shown up to turn his life upside down.

ANNIE SAT on one of the wicker porch chairs wrapped in a heavy blanket, the cup of coffee she held warming her hands. The sun was just rising, gilding the calm surface of the ocean. She'd had a restless night, worrying about Auntie G. and wondering about her own future. Living in Bisbee, waiting tables and making purses, had worked for these past years. But that wasn't how she wanted to spend the rest of her life. Geneva's legacy of the house gave her options she'd never been able to consider.

She'd missed college, of course. Maybe she could rent the cottage and move to a university town, work part-time and take some classes. She'd always hoped to go into fashion design. Was it too late?

She inhaled the fragrant steam rising from her coffee. No use spoiling these few weeks with idle speculation. There would be time enough for that after…after… She shrugged off the threatening tears.

Shorebirds roused and set up their hungry cries as they strutted on the beach and wheeled low over the swells in search of breakfast. Annie watched them until she finished her coffee. Reluctantly she got to her feet. Mornings were so traitorously full of promise.

In the kitchen, she set about making a bacon-and-cheese quiche, hoping she could tempt Geneva. While it baked, she ran upstairs for a quick shower. The oven timer went off just as she finished slipping into a sweatshirt and jeans. Racing into the kitchen, she shut off the timer and then checked on her great-aunt, who lay on her back staring at the ceiling, her breath labored.

"I've made something special for breakfast."

"Smells good, honey. But I'm not hungry."

"Let me help you sit up." Supporting Geneva, she plumped up the pillows and straightened her covers. "Better?"

"Thank you."

"I'll be right back with your breakfast tray."

Annie thought she heard Geneva sigh as she left the room. Had it been only a week ago that Geneva had dressed before breakfast and eaten at the kitchen table? Annie filled the teapot with boiling water, put a slice of quiche on a plate and added some leftover fruit salad. Carrying the tray with care, she set it down in front of Geneva, then spread the blue-and-white-checkered napkin over her chest.

"How did you sleep?"

Geneva made a fluttering motion with her hand. "I don't have time for sleep. Too much to think about."

Annie knew that wasn't totally true since Geneva spent an increasing amount of her days and nights dozing. "Like what?"

"The past." She lifted a tentative forkful of quiche to her mouth. "So many are gone." She chewed quietly as if reviewing the parade of friends and loved ones who had passed away.

Annie could empathize. When she'd left Eden Bay, it was not only Pete she'd left behind, but friends, now scattered to the four winds, and not likely to welcome her even if she located them.

"And about you."

Annie blinked. "Me?"

"You need people. Love."

"I have friends in Bisbee, and Nina has been like a second mother."

Geneva swirled the tea bag in the pot and, with shaking hands, poured herself a cup. "That's not the same."

"The same as what?"

"Having someone who cares deeply about your welfare."

Pete's adoring face swam before her eyes. "I know."

"It's time to think about the future, not dwell on the past."

Annie swallowed the lump in her throat. "I'm not sure I know how."

"Exactly my point. Before I march in with the saints, I intend to do something about that. If I can."

And what would that be? Annie hadn't a clue.

A loud knock on the door interrupted her reverie. "Just a minute, Auntie G. That must be Kyle Becker. Eat some more, please, while I'm gone."

For reasons she didn't want to examine, she paused before the hall mirror and ran a hand through her hair, wishing she'd put on some lipstick. When she opened the door, expecting to see Kyle, she stepped back in surprise.

"Good morning, ma'am." A stout older man with a beard stood on the porch. "I'm Vince Rayburn. Kyle sent me over to paint your porch. I just wanted to let you know I was here."

"Isn't he coming today?" She hated the disappointment she heard in her own voice.

"No, he's checking on some other jobs. Said it might be a day or two before he'd be back."

Annie thanked him and slowly closed the door,

furious with herself. She was actually upset that she wouldn't see Kyle. What was wrong with her? Deep down she knew the answer.

Kyle Becker made her heart race.

KYLE STRADDLED the bar stool, shoved the ball cap back on his head and ordered a lager. After work, he hadn't wanted to go home to his empty house. The Yacht Club, comforting in its familiarity, was at the same time vaguely depressing. The changes to the place since he and Pete had drunk their first legal beer here were that Ollie, the owner, now had gray hair, and a new flat-screen TV, tuned to a soccer rematch, dominated the area above the bar. The dimly lit interior, stale smells and loud music blaring from the small dance floor made him wonder why he'd sought this particular refuge. The truth was…he was in a rut.

"Here ya go." Ollie placed the pilsner glass in front of Kyle. "How's it hanging?"

By a thread, he wanted to say. "Great."

"Don't usually see you in here on a weeknight." Ollie made a show of wiping down the counter. "Problems?"

Nothing I'm going to share with you. "Nah. Just thirsty."

He could hardly tell Ollie about nightmares and betrayal. About the way soft hazel eyes avoided his or the lump in his throat whenever he thought about Pete and Annie. Or about the way he couldn't stop thinking about her, no matter how hard he tried. For years anger at the way she'd treated Pete had kept him sane, but every time he saw her now, it was harder to use resentment as a barrier.

He drained his beer and ordered another. People came and went, slapping him on the back and giving him high fives, but he declined their invitations to join them. When Shellie Austin, a bleached blonde he'd known since high school, settled at the adjacent bar stool, he knew he was supposed to be interested. Might have been even a few short weeks ago.

Suddenly everything—the woman, the bar, his life—seemed tedious beyond bearing. He stood, then laid several bills on the counter. "Hey, Shellie, your next drink's on me."

Outside, he leaned against the truck, pulling in deep breaths of fresh air. Was this what his life had come to?

Everything he'd ever wanted had always remained beyond his reach. A stable home with a mother and father who loved him. A lifelong friendship with his best buddy. And, difficult as it was to admit, a girl with hair like silk who loved another.

Climbing into his truck, he paused, taking in the garish, flashing neon sign—The Yacht Club—symbol of all that was shallow and meaningless in his life. Not even Bubba's enthusiastic greeting elevated his mood.

TWO MORE DAYS PASSED and still no Kyle. Two days during which Geneva struggled to complete the family history—filling in the blanks with anecdotes and more photographs.

By Thursday, Annie was increasingly concerned. Auntie G.'s feet were swollen, and she was eating like a bird and spending more time in bed. Most alarming were her spells of fighting for the next breath. Although her eyes were still bright with intelligence, now Annie noticed in them something she had never seen before—fear. After conferring on the phone with Carmen, Annie called the doctor, who scheduled a late-afternoon appointment.

Cajoling Geneva to eat the tiny portion of chicken salad she'd prepared for lunch, Annie heard a loud thump outside. She went out on the porch. There stood Kyle, fastening a tool belt around his waist. A tall ladder was propped against the side of the house. Annie momentarily closed her eyes against the relief she felt. Even if he hated her, his presence was oddly comforting. Familiar.

He lifted the Mariners ball cap and scratched his head. "Something I can do for you?"

"I, uh, I didn't know you were here, and when we heard the noise—"

"Oh. The ladder. Sorry about the racket. I should've knocked. There will be more commotion, I'm afraid. I'm fixing your roof today."

It was then she noticed the pile of shingles beneath her bedroom window.

Kyle's gray eyes bored into her. "Will that be a problem? I need to complete the work on the roof before I start tearing out the Sheetrock in your bedroom."

Was it just her or were they being overly polite with each other?

"My great-aunt sleeps quite a bit, but I suppose the repairs have to be made."

"I hope to get the roof under control today." He put

one foot on the first rung of the ladder, drawing his jeans tight across his butt.

Annie tried not to notice, just as she tried to ignore the breadth of his shoulders, the muscular, tanned arm grasping the fourth rung. Unaccustomed heat caused her to blush. His sheer masculinity unleashed long-stifled desire, the suddenness of it taking her aback. Embarrassed, she turned on her heels. "Do what you need to do," she said more curtly than she'd intended.

Once safely inside the house, she leaned over, hands on her knees, and took several deep breaths. What was she thinking? Her involuntary reaction to Kyle scared her. He was Pete's best friend. She couldn't allow herself—wouldn't allow herself to think of him that way. Even if Kyle were similarly attracted, which was highly unlikely, any attachment was unthinkable. Just as it had been on that strange May night at the end of their senior year.

It had been the week before graduation. Even though it was a cool night, a group of seniors had gone to the beach. Gathered around a roaring bonfire, they'd laughed and sung, until Kyle remarked that this might be one of the last times they'd all be together before they moved on to work and college. The mood turned somber and reflective. A few of the girls got teary, and Annie could remember wanting to hold on to the moment and never let it go.

Instead of scattering to their usual make-out places, the couples all remained by the fire, reminiscing. Pete had snuggled her close, reassuring her. "The best is yet to come," he whispered. "We'll have the rest of our lives together." She remembered feeling contentment and a sense of being luckier than most of her classmates.

After midnight when the last sparks of the fire died against the night sky, they'd slowly folded their blankets and ambled toward their cars. Pete was carrying a cooler, and Annie had started to follow him when she noticed Kyle standing apart near the breaking waves. Something about the way he stood there—so separate—broke her heart. Instead of following Pete and the others, she went over to Kyle and put a hand on his shoulder. "Are you all right?"

When he shrugged, she turned him toward her, astonished to see tears welling in his eyes. In the distance she heard the shouts of her friends, engines revving. But the beach felt deserted, except for the rhythm of the sea and the boy's naked, anguished expression. "Kyle?"

"Don't, Annie, just don't," he said gruffly.

"Please, what's wrong?"

Before she knew what was happening, he'd pulled her into his arms, holding her as if he'd never let her go.

Abruptly he'd flung her away. "That's what's wrong, damn it. You, Annie. You."

Then he'd walked off, leaving her standing there with a pounding heart and the slowly dawning realization of what had happened. There had been no mistaking the need in his eyes.

Kyle. Pete. They were best friends. And Kyle was her friend, too, but something had changed that night.

Other than at the graduation ceremony, she hadn't seen Kyle again until the day he'd knocked on Auntie G.'s door.

Dismissing the memory and its emotional impact, she

pulled herself together and returned to the living room and saw that, once again, Auntie G. had rearranged the food on her plate to make it look as if she had eaten something.

"You're not fooling me, you know."

Geneva shrugged. "I know you're trying. And the salad looks lovely, but I'm not hungry." She set her plate on the end table beside her chair.

Swallowing back the grief tearing at her throat, Annie said, "*Please,* Auntie G. Don't do this."

Geneva reached out a gnarled hand and drew Annie onto the floor beside her chair. "It's my time, dear. I'm doing what I can for your sake. But the day is coming when I will no longer be able to fight."

"I can't bear to lose you." Annie laid her head in Geneva's lap to conceal her tears.

"I know." Auntie G.'s gentle hand caressed Annie's head. "But dying is part of life. We're none of us given any promises, and I've lasted longer than most."

They sat like that for several minutes, suspended in a silence broken only by the wheeze of Geneva's oxygen tank and the intermittent sound of hammer blows on the roof.

IT TOOK over an hour to get Auntie G. dressed and ready to leave for the doctor's appointment. Twice she had changed her mind about what she wanted to wear, opting finally for a colorful yellow Mexican dress, which only served to emphasize her pale complexion. She spent considerable time at her dressing table and, with a trembling hand, applied mascara, rouge and lipstick. She completed her outfit with a turquoise and silver necklace. When she sat back to appraise the result in the mirror, she blew out a disgusted breath. "I look like hell."

As if to underline the comment, a loud blow sounded from the roof. In her imagination, Annie raised a fist and shook it at Kyle Becker. She had been fighting a headache all afternoon and didn't need any further aggravation.

Before they could leave, Geneva insisted on dumping the contents of her purse on the bed and selecting a different handbag. Rifling through her billfold, she located her insurance cards. Only then did she fill the new bag and pronounce herself ready. Glancing surreptitiously at her watch, Annie saw they would be cutting it close to make it on time.

"Wait here while I pull the car up to the door." Annie collapsed the wheelchair and stowed it in the trunk, then returned to help Geneva down the steps. Balancing herself with the walker and supported by Annie, who tucked an arm around her waist, Geneva started across the porch. Just then Kyle rounded the corner of the house carrying another load of shingles from his pickup. Dropping the shingles, he bounded toward them. "Here, let me help."

He handed Annie the walker before swooping Geneva up and heading for the car. Annie managed a smile when she heard her great-aunt say, "I always did fancy a strong man."

By the time she'd folded up the walker and stowed it and arranged the portable oxygen tank in the front seat, Annie was even more concerned about the time, knowing that she would face the cumbersome unloading process on the other end.

"Thank you," she murmured as she brushed past Kyle, his warm, metallic scent turning her knees to rubber.

He reached out and grabbed her arm. "Where are you going? Do you need me to follow you?"

She could hardly trust herself to look up, because she knew his eyes would be full of sympathy. And they were. "That's not necessary, but I appreciate the thought. Geneva has a doctor's appointment."

Before releasing her, he ran his hand down her arm, setting up goose bumps. "This can't be easy for you, Annie. You can ask for help, you know."

Ducking her head, Annie slithered behind the wheel. His thoughtfulness had unnerved her. Before closing the car door, she nodded. "I will if I need to," she said, praying she would never have to ask.

Kyle stood in the driveway watching Annie's vintage Honda lurch over the rutted road to the highway. Geneva Greer was light as a feather. In the short time he'd been working on the house, she had faded like a late-autumn bloom. Annie's devotion to her great-aunt was evident, but he could tell it was sapping her energy. In her oversize shirts and sweaters, she looked like a wraith trying to escape notice. This picture was at complete odds with the animated, sparkly eyed teen she'd been. Kyle wondered what it would take to restore the person he'd once known.

Why did he care? Shaking his head in bewilderment, he picked up the stack of shingles and moved them to the base of the ladder. A breeze gusted and the sharp tang of salt filled the air. Scanning the horizon, he saw a bank of dark clouds massing over the water.

Later, he didn't know whether he'd used the weather as his excuse or whether he'd been motivated by a different reason—one he didn't want to think about—but at the time, it had seemed as if there was only one decision to be made.

Kyle abandoned the roofing project, ran to his truck and followed the little Honda to the physicians' offices near the hospital.

ANNIE SIGHED gratefully when she pulled into the circular driveway and parked by the handicap access ramp. Already they were five minutes late for the appointment. She heaved the wheelchair from the trunk, unfolded it and positioned it by the passenger door, making sure to lock the wheels.

"Before, I could always walk in," Geneva said with a hitch in her voice, as she lowered herself into the waiting seat.

"Would you like me to bring your walker?"

"Please."

"Here it is." Startled by the deep, familiar voice, Annie wheeled around. Kyle waited at the rear of the trunk with the walker in his hand. "Got everything?"

Annie nodded mutely, and Kyle closed the trunk lid. Then he said, "Give me your keys. I'll park your car and bring the walker in. Just tell me which doctor."

Completely flustered by the fact Kyle had followed them, Annie mumbled, "Dr. Bari Woodruff," and handed him her keys.

Hooking the oxygen tank over the back of the wheelchair, Annie pushed Geneva toward the door. Even in her weakened condition, though, Auntie G. mustered the strength to say in a loud voice, "I think Mr. Becker is sweet on you, missy."

"You have an overly active imagination."

"I know what these old eyes tell me." Geneva raised her arm in a forward-march signal. "Now, for heaven's sake, let's get this over with."

Thankful for the reprieve from a conversation she didn't want to pursue, Annie pushed as fast as she safely could. Several people occupied chairs in the doctor's waiting room and the receptionist told them they would have to wait a few minutes. After a nurse came to take Geneva for some lab work, Annie collapsed onto a vinyl-covered sofa.

When the door opened and Kyle looked around the room, Annie waved. Spotting her, he set the walker against a wall and sat down beside her. Annie was both irritated and appreciative. It was getting more difficult to maneuver Geneva from place to place, but she didn't want anything from this man, especially not kindness.

"What exactly are you doing here?" she asked to break the awkward silence.

He put his arm on the back of the sofa and turned sideways to look at her. "The truth? Damned if I know. You just looked like you needed someone to lean on and I was there."

"I could've managed."

"I'm sure you could have. You enjoy your independence, don't you?"

There was an edge to his voice that made his meaning

clear: you liked it so much you walked away from Pete without a backward glance.

"What's wrong with that?"

"Look, Annie, I didn't come here to get into a verbal sparring match with you."

"Then back to my original question. What *are* you doing here?"

Before he could answer, a nurse called Annie's name. He gestured toward the wall. "Do you want the walker?"

Annie gathered it up. "Thank you. You don't need to wait." Eyes fixed on the nurse, whom she followed down the hall, she didn't look back.

If she had, she would have seen Kyle shrug, then pick up a dog-eared magazine and sit back down on the sofa.

The headlines swam: Middle East Violence Escalates, Six Panoramic Highway Drives, Male Menopause: Fact of Fiction?

Disgusted, Kyle threw down the magazine and leaned his head back. Annie had cut right to the quick. What was he doing here? He didn't normally think of himself as impulsive, but this was edge-of-the-cliff stuff. The woman haunted him—in his thoughts, in his dreams and, most especially, in the flesh. He could no more have stayed away when he'd seen her struggling with Geneva and all her paraphernalia than fly. And even as his gut clenched, he admitted to himself that it wasn't gallantry that had brought him here. No, something stronger and scarier. He wanted to protect Annie from the pain he knew was coming. Geneva Greer had returned to Eden Bay to die, and that would be a crushing blow for her great-niece.

He closed his eyes, oblivious to the conversations around him and to the comings and goings in the reception room. He could rationalize that he was doing this for Pete, knowing that his friend would have done anything to make life easier for Annie. In fact, thinking of Pete should help him get a grip on his inappropriate attraction to Annie.

But this wasn't about Pete. And it wasn't about the past. This was about Annie and him and now. Damned, though, if he knew what to do about any of it.

He felt a gentle hand on his shoulder and opened his eyes. "Kyle?" Annie stood in front of him, her lip trembling, her voice ragged.

He rose to his feet. She stood mere inches from him. "It's Auntie G." She paused, unable to go on. "They're…they're hospitalizing her. Dehydration, the doctor said. And other complications. Fluid buildup and…" She was unable to finish.

He couldn't help himself. He reached out and cradled her ravaged face in his hands. "I'm so sorry."

A sob choked her and she flung herself into his arms, dampening his shirt with her tears. "Oh, Kyle, what am I going to do?"

"Shh," he crooned. "Just let it go, Annie. Let it go."

As he stood there holding her in his embrace, breathing in her floral scent, feeling her chest heaving in the effort to take in air, he knew the answer to her question.

What was he doing here?

He held her even more closely. *This.* Simply and inevitably *this.*

CHAPTER FIVE

THE NEXT FEW HOURS PASSED in a daze of bureaucratic and clinical red tape. After waiting while Dr. Woodruff made arrangements for a bed at the small Eden Bay Hospital next door, Kyle helped Annie move Geneva to the medical facility before heading out. The forty-minute admission process grated on Annie's nerves and tired her great-aunt. When a room was finally available, Annie and a nurse undressed Geneva and helped her into bed. "I don't like this!" she complained. Further objections were cut off by a fit of coughing, administration of oxygen, insertion of IVs and attachment of monitors.

At a loss, Annie stood by as the nurses fussed over her aunt. Once they had her settled, one of them asked if Geneva had eaten dinner. Although the frail woman waved her hand dismissively, a tray arrived with a turkey sandwich, applesauce, butterscotch pudding, cranberry juice and a roll. "Hospital food. Bah."

Annie struggled to control her emotions. "You'd prefer to be fed intravenously?"

Auntie G. had the grace to appear contrite. "No, but—"

"No buts. You'll be hooked up to tubes if you don't do what you're told."

A wan smile crossed Geneva's lips. "Obedience. Not my strong suit."

"Tell me something I don't know."

Geneva managed the applesauce, half her pudding and one small bite of the roll. "I'm done."

"Try the juice."

Shooting Annie a disgusted look, she set about sipping from the cardboard container. "Where's that young man?"

"Kyle? He went home."

"It was nice of him to help us."

Annie tried not to think about just how nice he'd been, holding her protectively as her world fell apart. "Yes, it was."

"He likes you."

"Don't be ridiculous."

"I've been around the block a few times, remember? I know what I know."

Annie removed the meal tray and smoothed the sheets around Geneva, trying not to think about what her great-aunt had said. "Here's what I know. You need to rest. Let me lower the bed a bit."

"All right. Maybe I could sleep awhile." She closed her eyes for a minute or two, then opened them. "Go home. There's nothing you can do here."

Momentary panic cut off Annie's breath. "I want to be with you."

"Go home. Get some dinner. You could stand some rest yourself."

No matter how drained she was, Annie had every

intention of spending the night at the hospital. "All right. I'll grab a bite and change clothes, but I'll be back."

Geneva put up no argument—she was fast asleep. Annie watched her for several moments, thinking how frail she looked. Then, picking up her purse, she stole quietly from the room. When she passed the waiting room on the way to the elevator, she was stunned to see Kyle sprawled in a chair, a *Sports Illustrated* open in his lap. She paused in the doorway. "What are you doing here?"

He set the magazine aside and rose to his feet. "Isn't that question getting a bit repetitious?" He moved across the room and put an arm around her shoulders and walked her to the elevator. "I figured you hadn't eaten. Ms. Greer isn't the only one who needs to keep her strength up. I'm treating you to the best dinner the hospital cafeteria has to offer."

"I thought you went home."

"I did. Had to feed that dog of mine. But now I'm back."

The elevator pinged and she turned to face him. "Why?"

Standing with his back against the open elevator door, he let her enter first. He hesitated, his eyes fixed on hers. "You need me," he finally said. "Besides, against all the odds, I like you."

Annie lowered her head and focused on the waxed floor of the car. Kyle's words merely added to the confusion she was already feeling about him.

THE CAFETERIA FARE wasn't half-bad, Kyle thought, as he spooned up another forkful of lasagna. Annie had already finished half of a barbecued pork sandwich and was starting on her coleslaw. She caught him studying her and said, apologetically, "I was hungrier than I thought."

"You'll be of no use to your aunt if you don't take care of yourself."

"She's getting worse," Annie said quietly. "I don't know how much longer—"

"Whoa. One day at a time."

"I know, but it's so hard. She's all I have."

Tears flooded her eyes and, setting down her fork, she tried to hide her face behind her paper napkin. He knew Geneva Greer's condition justified Annie's concern, but sitting here, not being able to change things, made him feel helpless. He tried to lighten the mood by changing the subject. "Where did you come from when you returned to Eden Bay?"

"Bisbee, Arizona. I've lived there…for a long time."

"You have friends there?"

"A few."

"Somebody special?" He cursed himself for caring about her answer.

"A man?" She shook her head. "No. After Pete, I…" Like a cloud suddenly obscuring the light, a wounded expression came over her face and she stopped.

He knew they were skirting uncomfortably close to topics she didn't want to discuss—and which he desperately wanted to know about. "Pete was a pretty special guy."

"Could we please not talk about him?"

"Okay, but if we're trying to be friends again, we'll have to sometime."

"Not now!" Her shrill answer caused the nurses at the next table to turn and stare at her. Annie seemed to shrink within herself. "Please, Kyle, just leave it."

He nodded and then, without another word, finished his dinner.

"I'm sorry," Annie finally said, her tone conciliatory. "I know you're trying to help."

"How about I help some more by running you home to get whatever you need. I assume you plan to spend the night here. That way you can leave your car in the parking lot and I'll bring you back."

He was surprised when she didn't put up an argument. And even more surprised when she grabbed his arm as they walked to his truck, holding on as if to a lifeline. She said nothing on the way to the house. Only when he parked in the driveway did she turn to look at him. Then in a squeaky voice, her eyes wide and beseeching, she spoke, so quietly he had to strain to hear. "I've never talked about Pete. Ever. I think maybe—" she lowered her eyes, hesitating "—maybe I could. Just not now. Perhaps one day."

He picked up her icy hand and warmed it in his two. "I understand. Whenever you're ready."

Later, after he'd dropped her at the hospital and was driving home, he wondered what sorcerer's spell she had cast on him. Damn right, he'd wanted for years to talk about Pete and about her callous and ultimately fatal effect on him; but when he was with Annie, those angry thoughts deserted him, and he fell under the enchantment of her fragile beauty and vulnerability. She had gotten to him again. Big-time!

WIDE-AWAKE, Geneva lay listening to the rhythmic clicks and clacks of the equipment dedicated to keeping her alive. In the darkness, brightened only by a low-wattage lamp at the head of her bed, she could barely make out the IV stand and monitor, looming like robotic sentinels of death. Incredulity and rage flooded through her. She couldn't be dying now. And most certainly not in the impersonal confines of this hospital. That was not her plan.

Fumbling in the folds of her blanket, she located the remote control and raised the head of the bed a few notches, hoping to relieve the heaviness sitting on her chest like an anvil. Across the room, she noticed a cramped, pretzel-like body curled into a recliner. Annie. She should've known the child would insist on staying with her.

For over a year, she had known her days were numbered. Dying itself wasn't the problem. Annie was. The niece she adored was imprisoned by a past Geneva had yet to unravel. For that reason alone, she had to hang on. Getting at the truth would be painful for them both, but it had to be done. If that meant forcing down food, enduring respiratory therapy and conning her way out of the hospital, Geneva would do it.

As a little girl, Annie had been a ray of sunshine, flitting from flower to butterfly to abalone shell in sheer delight. John had doted on his daughter, and Liz loved having a little girl to dress in bows and ruffles. After her father's untimely death, Annie, with the intuitiveness of the young, had devoted herself to making her mother's life easier, happier. At a young age, she'd come home from school and prepared supper. She'd understood that excelling was a way to coax a smile from her mother. Geneva used to worry about the strain such efforts put on the girl. Dance recitals, cheerleading competitions, tennis matches—it didn't matter. In Liz's eyes, Annie had to be a star.

And what had been her reward? Her shallow mother's grudging approval, tainted by unrealistic expectations. Yet Annie had never stopped trying and somehow, through it all, never stopped being that ray of sunshine. Until…

Geneva would go to her grave wishing she had been in Eden Bay for Annie's high school graduation and regretting she had been unable to alter whatever events had scarred Annie so profoundly.

She glanced again at her great-niece, still sleeping, her head on her forearm. Soon. She would ask Annie soon. Force some answers from her. While she still could.

ANNIE WOKE to the early-morning bustle of the nurses' shift change. She straightened up in the chair and stretched her arms above her head, yawning. Then, realizing where she was, she hurried to Geneva's bedside. Her great-aunt lay with her head elevated, breathing raggedly, her eyes closed. Annie had never been much of a one for prayer, especially to a deity who had failed her before, but in the half-light filtering into the room, she raised her eyes to whatever god might be looking down on them, and whispered, "Please. Not yet."

Finally, needing caffeine, she left Geneva. At the courtesy station, she fixed a cup of coffee, thankfully fresh and strong. Reentering Auntie G.'s room, Annie found two nurses hovering over their patient, one of them changing the IV, the other reviewing the chart.

With a start, Geneva awoke, her eyes frantically scanning the room. "Annie?"

"I'm here, Auntie G. It's all right. The nurses are checking on you, that's all."

"Tell them not to bother. I'm going home today."

"Now, Ms. Greer," one of the nurses said, "That's for Dr. Woodruff to decide."

Geneva blew a disgusted raspberry. "Like hell," Annie thought she heard her mutter.

When the nurses finished their duties, one of them, a plump, redheaded woman dressed in a purple flowered scrub suit, lingered. "Excuse me," she said, laying a hand on Annie's shoulder. "You must be Annie Greer."

Annie looked into the nurse's sympathetic blue eyes. There was something familiar in the lines of the woman's face. "Yes. Do I know you?"

"It's been so long, I don't know if you'll remember me. I'm Carolee Huxley. Well, I used to be. Now I'm Carolee Nordstrom."

In her mind, Annie flipped the pages of her high school yearbook, and then memory clicked in. "Wow! It's been a few years since Mrs. Cole's dance classes." They'd met in ninth grade when she and Carolee had performed a duet for their recital. The pleasure of recognition faded as soon as Annie realized that in Carolee's mind, she was probably still not welcome in Eden Bay.

Carolee nodded toward the bed where Geneva had gone back to sleep. "I'm so sorry we have to reconnect under these circumstances. Rest assured, Ms. Greer will get the best possible care."

Was that the nurse's way of dismissing her ties to Annie? "I appreciate that."

Cocking her head, Carolee said, "You've been gone from here a number of years, right?"

"Since high school graduation," Annie murmured, hoping Carolee would not recall her abrupt departure.

"Have you been in touch with any of the gals in our class?"

More than anything, Annie wanted this conversation to end. "No."

"I don't mean to be presumptuous, but maybe you could use someone to talk to." Her glance took in Geneva. "This is a difficult situation. If you'd let me, I'd like to help. Would you be available to meet me in the cafeteria for a quick lunch, say, around one-thirty?"

If you'd let me? Surely Carolee wasn't trying to befriend her. Or maybe she was ignorant of what had happened with Pete. What if she didn't know? Would she still want to renew their acquaintance when she found out?

Carolee stepped back. "If you'd rather not—"

Annie recovered her manners. "No, it's not that at all." She hesitated, wondering whether to risk the connection. When she looked at Carolee, the woman's eyes mirrored both confusion and understanding. "Yes. Thanks. I'll be there at one-thirty."

"Great, see you then. Now if you'll excuse me, it's back to the Florence Nightingale routine."

When Carolee left the room, Annie wandered to the window. A fog bank hung low over the ocean and beaches, but sunshine dappled the buildings and parking lot below. She knew the sun would eventually win, burning off the fog. The metaphor hit close to home. If only the fog in her life could be so easily and naturally dissolved.

After a few moments, she returned to Auntie G.'s bedside. Pulling up a chair, she sat quietly holding Geneva's hand.

"A friend?"

Annie stood, leaning closer. "Who?"

"That nurse."

"Someone I used to know. That's all."

Auntie G.'s eyes flew open. "No! That's not all. You need a friend. Never turn your back on such an opportunity."

Annie smiled weakly, "I won't," she said, even as she wondered whether she could trust the friendship of anyone in Eden Bay.

Dr. Woodruff made rounds midmorning. After reading the chart and examining Geneva, she beckoned Annie to follow her into the hall. "She's insisting on going home."

"I know."

The doctor's expression reflected her concern. "We're better able to care for her here. On the other hand, I have to take her wishes into consideration."

Annie's heart thumped in recognition of what the doctor wasn't saying. "How long does she have?"

"That's hard to predict. Cases vary. But even given that window of uncertainty, not long. We can keep her a few days and build up her strength. If she insists on returning home, how would you feel about having twenty-four-hour nursing care when it all becomes too much for you?"

"Frankly? Relieved. If she wants to die at home, that is my wish, as well. Money isn't an object."

"I can only imagine how hard this is for you. She's a valiant lady." The doctor plucked a pen from the pocket of her lab coat and made a notation on the chart. "I'll send up a social worker to talk with you later this morning."

The wheels are in motion, Annie thought, as she watched the doctor walk briskly down the corridor. And she was powerless to prevent the inevitable.

WALKING OUT of the office toward his truck, preoccupied with thoughts of Geneva Greer, Annie and the day ahead, Kyle was surprised when Pete's sister Margaret stepped out of her parked SUV. "Got a minute?" She stood stiffly, arms wrapped protectively around her waist.

Kyle shrugged. "Sure. What's up?"

Margaret glanced around the parking lot as if fearful of discovery. "This won't take long. Could we talk in your truck?"

He let Bubba out and held the door for her. "Be my guest." She sat in the passenger seat, hands folded, her fingers working nervously.

Rounding the back of the vehicle, Kyle wondered what this was about. Margaret, the mother of two children, rarely came to Nemec Construction and even more rarely engaged him in more than perfunctory conversation.

Once in the truck, he turned to face her, his arm draped over the steering wheel. "Well?"

She didn't bother with pleasantries. "I want to know about Annie Greer."

The question was loaded. Keeping his tone neutral, Kyle said, "What exactly are you talking about and why me?"

"You, because you've been around her pretty constantly. And what exactly? How dare she come back here and stir up all these memories? It was easy enough for her to prance out of my brother's life without so much as a fare-thee-well. Never a word, a letter, a phone call. Nothing. She broke Pete's heart and never looked back. The thought of her being here in Eden Bay makes me sick."

Kyle took a deep breath. Margaret's anger was palpable—and understandable. She was eighteen months older than Pete, and they had always been extremely close. She had been his champion, supporting him in athletics, paving the way for him with teachers and delighting in his brotherly pranks, even when she herself was the target. Pete's death had devastated all of the Nemecs, but Margaret had had a particularly rough time accepting the reality of it and she'd never forgiven Annie for causing Pete so much pain.

"She's in town to care for Geneva Greer."

"I know that. But wouldn't you think since she's shown up, she'd have the decency to tell us why she blew Pete off and left him heartbroken? Any caring person, *anyone,* would have had the decency to put him out of his misery and explain to him why she'd left in such a hurry. He's not here to listen to whatever her story is, but we are. She owes us at least that. And then she needs to leave Eden Bay and never come back."

What was there to say? Kyle had nursed those same thoughts. Why had Annie disappeared without any word to the young man she had claimed to love? In some ways, he wished he could lose himself in righteous indignation the way Margaret had, but then Annie's face swam before him, and he knew their relationship was far beyond a simple solution. "What is it you're wanting from me, Margaret?"

She buried her head in her hands. "I don't know." Seconds passed. "Maybe I'm hoping that if I just had an explanation, I could move on. But…" Her voice trailed off. When she lifted her head, her face was streaked with tears. "I miss Pete so much."

Steeling himself against the ache in his chest, he laid a hand on her shoulder. "So do I. Every day."

She turned toward him, her face ravaged. "Then how can you spend time with *her?*"

It was a question he'd asked himself. Was there an explanation? Not one that would satisfy the grief-stricken woman sitting beside him. "She's hurt, too."

An incredulous look hardened Margaret's features. "Give me a break, Kyle. Don't tell me you're falling into her trap?"

Was that what it was? A trap? "Wait and see, Margaret. Right now Annie's consumed with caring for her great-aunt. Maybe, with time…"

"Right. And I believe in the Easter bunny, too." She swiped a hand across her face. "I'm sorry to have burdened you. I was out of line." She grabbed the door handle.

He stopped her. "Don't apologize, please. Grief happens. I know that all too well. But give it more time, okay?"

As she left the truck, all he heard her say was "Whatever."

CAROLEE WAS a few minutes late and breezed into the cafeteria, full of apology. "Sorry to keep you waiting, but we had a last-minute emergency."

"Not…"

"Oh, dear, no. Not your great-aunt. In fact, her friend Frances is with her now." She turned and eyed the serving line. "What looks good?"

"The special today is meat loaf. You eat here often. What's your opinion?"

"First-class comfort food. Let's go. I'm starving!"

The special came with potatoes and gravy and green beans. Back at their table, Annie stared at her plate, not sure if she could eat a bite. What did Carolee know about her? About Pete?

"My kids don't like meat loaf, so this is a real treat." Carolee was clearly having no difficulty eating.

Annie asked about her children, then managed a few bites of the remarkably good meat loaf while Carolee bragged about her three sons and her husband, who was a physical therapist. It was hard to resist Carolee's amusing descriptions of her family and her hearty laugh. Gradually Annie found herself relaxing, caught up listening to Carolee, who finally paused and said, "Well, enough about me." She set down her fork and leaned forward. "I'm so glad you're back, Annie. I've thought of you often through the years. A confession.

When we were dance partners, I so wanted to be your new best friend."

"You did? I think I would've loved that. Why weren't we?"

"Um, I don't quite know how to put this. Oh, what the heck. Frankly, I don't think your mother thought I was quite good enough for you."

Annie's mouth dropped. "Oh, Carolee, I'm so sorry. What made you think that?"

"My mother invited you to my fifteenth birthday party."

"I don't remember that at all."

"For good reason. You weren't there. I've always suspected your mother intercepted the invitation. Anyway, she called and said that you couldn't come, but didn't give any reason. And you never said anything about it."

"I'm so sorry. I would love to have come." Annie shoved back her half-eaten plate. "Unfortunately, that sounds like my mother."

"Well, that's in the past. The thing is, I'm really glad we've reconnected."

Annie tensed. Carolee didn't know about Pete. She couldn't. Annie would be as thoughtless as her mother if she let this charade continue. Beneath the table, she wrung her napkin into a coil. "You realize I left Eden Bay right after graduation."

"Sure. And broke Pete Nemec's heart."

Annie gulped. "You know?"

"Everyone does. But, Annie, that was years ago. We've all moved on. I hope you have, too."

Annie sat in stunned silence. Was it possible, just possible, that there were others in Eden Bay who had moved on, as well? Who might, someday, be able to forgive her?

"Annie, what's the matter?"

Damn. She didn't want to cry here in the middle of the cafeteria. "You're being so very kind. I...I..."

"Why wouldn't I be?"

If you only knew. "Being back in Eden Bay is very difficult for me."

"I understand. Your aunt—"

"Beyond that. Not all of my memories of this place are good." She felt the truth bubbling up, choking her. But this was not the time, not the place. Carolee's sympathy was weakening her defenses.

"Do you want to talk about that sometime?"

"No!" Annie's stomach cramped. "I mean, I'm sorry. You've been so understanding, but I've worked through all of that." *Liar, liar, liar!*

"Enough said. On a lighter subject, I've enjoyed our lunch together. I'm wondering if we could do it again sometime?"

Carolee's acceptance of her made Annie long for what might have been. "Maybe."

Carolee gathered the remains of her lunch onto her tray and stood. "I need to get back." Then she paused and smiled at Annie. "You call me. Anytime."

Then she was gone. Annie sat nursing her iced tea. She couldn't remember when she had felt such warmth and welcome. A far cry from her encounter with Margaret on the beach. Carolee was offering friendship—something Annie desperately wanted. But how could she risk it?

KYLE HAD THOUGHT he would enjoy working on the Greer cottage roof with no one at home. He was wrong. All day he'd felt unsettled, expecting Annie to come out the door at any moment or Geneva to remind him of one more exacting task he needed to complete. The old lady had endeared herself to him on that very first visit when she had shared her commitment to maintaining the craftsmanship of the place. Her demise would be the end of an era. Not many of these early coastal houses were still in the hands of their original owners, and certainly few people had much interest in preserving the houses as they once were. These days it was more about adding a workout room or floor-to-ceiling glass on the ocean side.

He gave a final tap of the hammer at the ridge line, then sat back, legs outstretched, to watch the sunlight play over the whitecaps crashing against the rocky shoreline. A view like this was beyond price.

He was loading his gear into the truck bed and letting Bubba stretch his legs when he noticed Annie's Honda cresting the rise. She had to be exhausted. As she got out of the car, she gave him a weak wave. Coming toward him, she looked defenseless and forlorn, and every single one of his protective instincts surfaced.

He kicked at a pebble. He felt sorry for her, sure, but he had to put a lid on his feelings. Even without his encounter with Margaret this morning, he knew that being around Annie was dangerous. Everything argued against any involvement with her—his loyalty to Pete, his position with the Nemecs and especially his anger with her for walking out on Pete all those years ago. It would take more than a pitiful whimper to defuse that. If she could be so cavalier about leaving Pete high and dry, wouldn't she treat Kyle the same way?

He waited, color rising to his face. The more he tried to put a lock on his emotions, the more intense they became. She stopped in front of him. He steeled himself. He wouldn't, no, he wouldn't, put his arms around her. The wind stiffened and she hugged herself.

"Well?" he finally said.

She pulled up the hood of her sweatshirt and shrugged. "The news isn't good."

"How do you mean?"

She looked at the sky then straight back at him, her eyes brimming with tears. "I'm bringing her home to die."

Afterward, replaying the scene on his way home, he wondered what in hell had happened to his resolve, his high-and-mighty thoughts about steering clear of Annie Greer. All he knew was that no power on earth could have kept him from gathering her into his arms and rocking her in rhythm with the surf and the storm of her sobs.

Finally, her emotions under control, she'd invited him in, fixed sandwiches and told him about the plans to bring her great-aunt home and about her chance meeting with Carolee. No sooner had they finished eating than he could see she was anxious to return to the hospital.

He'd walked her to her car. "If there's anything you need, anything I can do..." His words hung impotently in the cool night air.

"I'll be fine," she assured him. Neither one of them believed her.

"Here," he said, digging out his business card. "Let me give you my home contact information, too." He scribbled his home address and phone number. "But you can almost always reach me on my cell."

"You don't have to go to all this trouble on my account."

"If Pete were here, it's what he'd do."

She gazed out to sea. The name echoed in the silence. Pete—the issue that lay between them, the pain that never went away.

When she turned back to Kyle, her eyes were clear, her shoulders straight. Then she'd left for the hospital without saying goodbye.

Before he even got into bed that night, Kyle knew the dream would come, insistent and unrelenting. He saw Bubba, sprawled at the foot of the bed, waiting for him, and Rita's words came back to taunt him. Yep, for a bed partner, he had a beast, not a woman. Honesty, like a knife, sliced through him. The only woman he wanted was off-limits to him. Annie Greer.

Kyle counted sheep long after Bubba was snoring contentedly. Then he tried counting backward from a thousand by sevens. Still, his muscles remained tense, his eyes grainy. Wanting Annie was like coveting your brother's wife. Not acceptable. He knew that. He knew, too, that none of this made any sense. The very last woman on earth to whom he should be attracted was the love of Pete's life.

And until he knew what had really happened between Pete and Annie, he could not allow his feelings to take control. But would she ever tell him? If she never did, then all this sleeplessness and preoccupation was an exercise in futility.

Finally, his eyes closed and he could feel himself descending into the black hole of sleep.

At three in the morning, he awoke with a jolt and sat up in bed, his face drenched, the clunk of the ax falling on Pete's neck reverberating in his brain. He went into the bathroom and doused his head under cold water. Slowly the room came into focus and the nightmare faded to gray, then black. He stood staring into the mirror, his eyes sunk deep into his face.

Okay, okay. He'd put it off long enough. He returned to the bedroom and flicked on the small lamp on his dresser. Opening the third drawer, he searched with his fingertips under his socks. At the back of the drawer, he finally felt it. The edge of an envelope. Extracting it from the drawer, he dropped it on the dresser top. Its wrinkles and smudges bore mute witness to the fact it had been carried around in his pocket for many months. Through the years, Kyle had done his damnedest not to think about what was inside.

Pete had pressed it on him before they shipped out for Afghanistan. "Just in case, buddy. Please. She's out there somewhere. I know it. Please, just hold on to it. If something happens to me, someday maybe the time will be right and you'll find her and deliver it."

Kyle closed his eyes against the memory of their ensuing argument. "Number one," he'd said, "give it up. She's out of your life, man. Number two, nothing is going to happen to you."

But it had. And here the letter was, lying accusingly on his dresser. Kyle stared at the two words written on the front in Pete's familiar block printing: *For Annie.*

When she had first come back to Eden Bay, Kyle had been too angry to give it to her, figuring she didn't deserve it.

Now he was afraid to give it to her. Afraid it would upset the delicate balance between them.

But Pete's memory demanded it.

CHAPTER SIX

KYLE GAVE UP on going back to sleep and headed for work around seven. The office was open until noon on Saturdays, providing a good time to process paperwork. On his way, he stopped at the doughnut shop for coffee and, figuring he deserved a reward for his sleepless night, overdosed on three maple sticks. It was dark and quiet when he let himself into the office. That suited him fine. He settled in his cubicle, Bubba at his feet, and dug into the stack of work orders needing his approval.

Then he turned to the specs for a clinic remodel his dentist had asked him to work up. He was running a few numbers on his calculator when a shadow fell across his desk.

"You're an early bird today."

He'd know that chirpy voice anywhere. He swiveled in his chair and looked up at Rosemary Nemec, dressed in a crisp pink tee and striped miniskirt, beaming down at him. A bubbly morning person, he thought to himself. Just what he needed after the night he'd had.

Doing his best not to growl, he said, "Good time to catch up."

She leaned over to study the specs, brushing her

breast against his shoulder in the process and shrouding him in a cloud of citrusy cologne. "Dr. Adams's office?"

"Yeah. I'm trying to figure a way to give him a decent estimate."

She pointed a carefully manicured finger at the plans. "Why don't you incorporate this bookcase into the receptionist's desk?"

He thought about it for a moment. "Yeah, that might just work." He shoved his chair away from her, hoping she'd take the hint and leave. "Thanks, Rosemary."

Instead, she folded her arms across her chest and leaned against his desk, still smiling the happy little grin she wore most of the time. "I, uh, was wondering. Are you busy next Friday night?"

His heart sank. "Why? You have something in mind?"

"I'm hoping. Dad and Mother bought a table for the country club dance benefiting the library. I thought we might go together. That is, if you'd like."

He'd rather do almost anything else. Maybe this was the time to get their relationship straightened out.

Before he could say anything, she went on. "Perhaps it was presumptuous, but I've already told Mom and Dad we'd love to come. I know I should've asked you first, but they were so pleased. Do say yes."

He hated being manipulated. "I don't know—"

"Oh, please." She stood up and put a hand on his shoulder.

He gritted his teeth against the imploring look in her eyes. He always felt out of place at the country club and had no romantic interest in Rosemary. She'd make some man an adoring and dutiful wife. But what did he need with adoring and dutiful? Okay, so maybe he'd go with her this one last time, use it as an opportunity to let her down gently, if that was possible.

"When shall I pick you up?"

Her body coiled with excitement and he feared she would actually jump up and down. Jeesh!

"Thanks, Kyle. You're the greatest." Then she leaned over and kissed him on the cheek. "Oh, seven. Yes, seven will be perfect." She favored him with one last blinding smile before heading for her desk.

Perfect? Awkward as hell, that's what it would be. He stuffed the specs back in a folder, pulled on his ball cap and whistled to Bubba. "C'mon, pup. Let's get out of here."

Fuming, he strode toward his truck. What was the matter with him? Here was a great girl practically throwing herself at him. But no. He had to make life difficult by obsessing about a woman who infuriated him, inspired guilt and shame, and, at the same time, made him want to chuck everything and carry her off into the sunset. Go figure.

DR. WOODRUFF KEPT Geneva in the hospital three more days. Annie worked at home in the mornings finishing the last of the purses for the Scottsdale boutique and found that losing herself in the designs and fabrics provided peace and a sense of normalcy, even if only briefly. Her work and early-evening walks on the beach were what kept her going.

Kyle had continued working on the house, even over the weekend, wanting to surprise Geneva with his progress when she returned. To that end, he spent several hours a day working inside replacing window jambs, refinishing wood trim and leveling the kitchen floor. When he was there, Annie either fled to her room or left for the hospital. She couldn't come to depend upon him. Accepting his help during her great-aunt's crisis was one thing, but relying on him, taking comfort in his presence—that was not advisable. No, she would pour all of her attention and energy into caring for Geneva and try to forget Kyle and the unaccustomed and disturbing feelings he aroused in her.

She had just finished putting a zipper in one of the purses when Kyle knocked on her bedroom door. "May I come in?"

She cursed the pleasant flutter in the vicinity of her chest. *Control, Annie, control.* "Yes."

When the door opened, the pure male scent of sawdust, sweat and varnish preceded him. "Hope I'm not disturbing you, but I need to look at your ceiling."

"No, I was just finishing some work." She shoved the handbag aside.

Kyle crossed the room and picked it up. "Hey, what's this? It's really nice. Did you make it?"

Against her will, Annie found herself warming to his interest. "I make one-of-a-kind purses for a shop in Arizona."

He examined it. "I'm no fashion expert, but I would imagine there'd be a big demand for stuff like this."

"This is a recent venture for me. But so far, so good."

He looked at her appraisingly, then grinned. "I always suspected you were more than just a pretty face."

A pretty face? Her glance swept briefly to the mirror over the dresser. No makeup, freckles, hair tied back in a scrunchie. But that was okay. It had been a long time since she'd worried about her looks. Not since that awful night. "It's work I love to do."

"That's obvious." He set the bag down. "Well, good for you. Now, then—" he studied the ceiling "—when would be a good time for me to tackle this?"

"I'm picking Geneva up at the hospital around noon tomorrow. Maybe you could work here in the morning. That way you wouldn't disturb her when she gets home."

"Deal. Except for one thing. Do you need me to go with you to get her?"

"They'll help me at the hospital, and if you're here when we get home and I need you, I'll let you know."

"Okay, then."

End of conversation, but he didn't leave the room. Annie felt heat rising to her cheeks. He was staring at her, his mouth curved in a gentle smile, his eyes warm. Then he reached out and tucked a flyaway wisp of hair behind her ear, his fingers grazing her cheek. Rooted to the spot, she was helpless to fight the attraction—no, the need—surfacing in her.

"Annie, I know these next few days aren't going to be easy for you. But when you feel yourself, well, uh…I guess I'm trying to say, I'm here for you."

He was being so nice. Pete's image rose in her mind. Pete, the one person she had always known she could count on, the one who had promised to be there for her always. What had she ever done to deserve two such good men in her life? And how it had pained her to devastate the one. Now, if she wasn't very, very careful, she would almost surely hurt the other. "Thank you for your concern, Kyle, but I'm prepared to handle everything."

The light faded from his eyes and he nodded. "Have it your way."

After he left, Annie crumpled into the chair at her workstation and buried her head in her arms, so tired, so very tired. Despite her good intentions, she'd managed to hurt Kyle. Increasingly, everything about him reminded her of that last bittersweet spring in Eden Bay. She couldn't indulge in such morbid trips down memory lane. She was going to need every ounce of strength to endure these precious final hours with Auntie G.

DAMN IT, damn it, damn it! Kyle knew he was hammering with more force than necessary, but physical activity had always been his emotional release. Annie was so friggin' independent. He didn't expect her to fall into his arms or gush with gratitude, but somebody needed to be there to help her through these next few days, and it looked as if fate had elected him. He sat back on his feet and rolled his eyes skyward. *Pete, if my relationship with Annie is one of your jokes, it isn't funny.*

But it would be just like Pete to arrange this—to see that the love of his life was taken care of. *Pick somebody else, please. I'm getting in too deep.*

He resumed nailing, wondering how much longer he could keep his hands off Annie. A sympathetic hug was one thing; the sexual stirrings she aroused in him were quite another. He had spent way too much time imagining what was hidden under her baggy shirts and bib overalls—round, pert breasts and firmly rounded buttocks. Crap! He was getting hot just thinking about it. The soulful quality of her expressions and the elfin grace of her movements were irresistible. Everything about her made him want to protect her and, at the same time, to explore all that lay beneath the surface.

But resist he must. Just as he'd told Bubba this morning, women were too damn much trouble!

TUESDAY AFTERNOON Geneva lay back in her own bed relishing the comfort of familiar surroundings. She'd take just a little snooze and then rally to sit in her chair by the living room window. She could breathe just as well—or just as poorly—there as lying here. Every day was a gift, despite the coughing fits and shortness of breath.

Dr. Woodruff had done her best with nutrients and medications, but Geneva could feel herself slowly drying into a husk of a person. Yet her thoughts raced. So much to remember. So many good times and interesting people, most of them dead now. Hers had been a rich and full life. Once a friend had asked if she'd ever regretted not having a husband. She'd come close to marrying a time or two, but reason had prevailed. Her feet were too itchy and her curiosity too vast to be confined for a lifetime by another's, even a beloved's, expectations. Each man in her life had brought different gifts—drop-dead handsome Pablo, the crazy Spaniard, with his easy laugh and sense of mischief; Reggie, dear Reggie, a public school Brit through and through, whose quick mind fascinated her; and then Whit, an

America's Cup–caliber yachtsman who spared no expense in providing her with beautiful things. She'd had her share of lovers and had enjoyed their minds and their bodies. All in all, not a bad life. One she was content to leave...except for Annie.

She must've slept for a while because the next thing she knew, Annie was standing by her bed, holding out the telephone. "Who is it?"

"I think you'll be pleased. It's Carmen."

Hearing the soothing accent of her housekeeper and companion was a tonic. Even better was the news that Carmen was coming for a visit the first of the week. When Geneva offered to pay for her airline ticket, Carmen demurred. "No, no, *señorita*. My daughter and her husband thank you so much for letting me come to help take care of the little one. They want to do this for me and for you."

"Please tell them thank you. I shall so look forward to our time together."

They talked a bit further, then hung up, but not before Carmen's mellifluous voice uttered words that suddenly carried far more significance than ever before. *"Vaya con Dios, amiga,"* she said at the end of their conversation.

Annie took the phone from her, a smile brightening her face. "That's good news, isn't it?"

"The best, petunia." She levered herself up in bed. "Now, I'm getting up."

"But don't you think—"

"I am not an invalid. I want to sit by my window and watch the birds and the clouds and the sea." She swung her legs over the side of the bed. "And where is that young man?"

"Kyle?"

"Yes. I want him to show me everything he's done so far. I like that boy. He's a hard worker."

"He's gone for the day, but he said he'll be back in the morning. He's done good work, I think."

Geneva shoved her feet into her slippers and hoisted herself to her feet. "Please bring me the wheelchair."

As Annie lowered her into the seat and draped a blanket over her knees, she said, "You're sounding pretty feisty this afternoon."

"I'm feeling better. Maybe I'll lick this thing yet." The words were brave and, for the moment, true. She did feel better than she had several days ago. But she knew it was a temporary reprieve.

Annie settled her by the window, fixed her a cup of tea and then disappeared into the kitchen to start dinner. The setting sun glared into the window. In earlier days, Geneva would have pulled the shade, but not today. Now she wanted to soak up every single ray of that incandescent ball slowly descending toward the horizon, before it sank into the sea, leaving behind only darkness.

It was right that Carmen was coming. She had been an integral part of Geneva's life for nearly twenty years, traveling with her, laundering, cooking, generally making her life easier. They knew each other's habits and understood when to give the other privacy. Their friendship had been choreographed by habit and proximity, but the time had come to say their goodbyes.

Geneva managed to eat most of the chicken breast,

potatoes and peas that Annie had fixed and then held on
for one game of gin rummy, which her great-niece won
handily. However, her mind wasn't really on the game,
but rather on choosing a time to talk with Annie about
the reasons for her flight to Bisbee all those years ago.
She was too tired tonight, and tomorrow Kyle Becker
would be here. She acknowledged to herself that as
much as this conversation needed to happen, she'd been
delaying it. Making Annie any more miserable than she
already was was going to be hard. But ignoring her
niece's pain and emotional paralysis was irresponsible.
And so few days remained.

KYLE MOVED carefully through the living room, not
wanting to disturb the old woman dozing in her chair.
Adding a coat of stain to the mantelpiece was relatively quiet work. Settling down to the task, he
became aware of movement from the work area in
Annie's bedroom. He imagined her hands playing
over fabrics. He'd been impressed by her purses. As
she'd told him about them, he'd recognized the enthu-
siasm that had been so much a part of her when they
were younger. She'd had a spark back then—a spark
he would love to ignite again under his own fingers.
He shut his eyes briefly, willing away that distracting
line of thought.

Half an hour later he put the lid on the can of stain
and carried his materials into the hallway, where he set
them down, pausing there to watch the rise and fall of
Geneva Greer's labored breathing and wishing he'd
gotten to know her sooner. Lost in his thoughts, he

didn't hear Annie come down the stairs. When she brushed past him bent on checking on Geneva, his gut clenched. Soon, too soon, Annie would be alone in the world. How had this happened? Why wasn't Pete here to soften the blow? Could anyone ever fill the void Geneva would leave? Could he?

He watched Annie adjust the blanket around Geneva's legs, then stand back, silent, as if willing her great-aunt to keep breathing. When she turned back toward him, eyes filled with tears, she seemed surprised he was still there. When he held out his arms, she swiped away the tears and shook her head, whispering fiercely, "No, Kyle."

He should have obeyed her, should have left the room. But a force beyond his control took over. "Annie, love, please." He drew her into his arms, holding her tight, running his hand over her head. "I know, I know," he murmured.

She stilled within his embrace, then laid her head against his chest, all the fight drained out of her. "It's so hard," she finally managed, her voice thick with pent-up tears.

He didn't know how long they stood like that—connected by a grief too great to bear...and by something more. Feelings that were too strong for either of them to deny. It was only when the grandfather clock struck three that she pulled away. They stood mute, for there were no words for such a moment.

Then, clearing his throat, Kyle picked up his tools and started for the truck, knowing that something momentous had just happened.

GENEVA WAS FRUSTRATED. She'd been home three days now and was still weak as a kitten. She let her fingers play over the satin border of the cashmere blanket she'd had for so many years. She needed to rest, but her mind wouldn't stop working. She kept thinking about Kyle and the pride he took in his craftsmanship. In these days and times, it was difficult to find a worker with high standards and a good work ethic.

It was even more difficult to find a good man. Rousing from her sleep earlier in the week, she had watched as Kyle tenderly embraced Annie, comforting her without words. When he had left the house, she had observed Annie move to the window, watching the man until she finally turned away, a stray tear dampening her cheek. But it was the expression on Annie's face that moved Geneva so deeply. Love, pure and simple.

Annie was on her usual Friday run to the grocery store. Geneva seized the opportunity and invited Kyle to join her by the bay window. She gazed out at the sea, puzzling how to gain the information she needed. He sat quietly, hands clasped between his knees. She liked that—a man who didn't need to fill the silence with unnecessary talk.

"You knew Annie in high school?" she began abruptly.

"Yes."

"Well?"

"Pete, her boyfriend, was my best friend. We hung out together quite a bit."

"Is she the same now as you remember her?"

She scrutinized him as he obviously struggled for

words. He rubbed his hands over the faded surface of his jeans, his eyes averted. She waited.

"No," he finally said.

"What's different?" She, of course, knew the myriad ways Annie had changed, but she wanted to hear what he'd noticed.

"I assume you have a reason for asking."

"Yes, I do. More about that later." She waited, the *tapeta, tapeta* of her oxygen marking the seconds that passed.

"Okay. I'm not a poetic kind of guy, as you might guess. But Annie back then, well, she was like a sunbeam. Wherever she went, people warmed to her. She wouldn't have been voted Homecoming Queen if she hadn't been well liked. You rarely saw her without a smile. She and Pete were the golden couple, the kind everybody just knew would walk off into the sunset and still be as much in love at the fiftieth high school reunion as they ever were." He winced, and a pained look replaced the thoughtful one.

"Enviable."

"Oh, yeah."

Geneva could see the toll this interrogation was taking on the young man, but she persevered. "And now? How does she seem to you?"

"Closed up. Private." His eyes sought Geneva's. "And needy." His obvious discomfort confirmed her hope that Kyle Becker had more than a passing interest in Annie.

She nodded in agreement. "I'm worried about her. Worried about what she'll do when I'm gone."

"She's pretty fragile."

"I think she's been that way since she left Eden Bay so suddenly." She hesitated, then forged on. "Do you have any idea what happened to make her run away like that?"

"You mean you don't know?"

"I have some ideas, but she won't talk about it. It's as if those memories are locked in a vault."

"At the time, I was very angry with Annie. Pete never got over her."

Geneva saw a glimmer of hope. "'At the time...'? What about now?"

She detected a faint flush rising from the open collar of his shirt. "Ms. Greer, have we finally come to the point of this conversation?"

She mentally gave him a high score for perceptiveness. "I could go any day now. No, no—" she raised her hand to fend off his objections "—for myself I'm as ready as a person can be. Annie has a few friends in Bisbee, but I need to know that she has at least one here in Eden Bay." She fixed her eyes on his, praying for the best. "Can I count on you, Kyle?"

He reached over and took her hand, but, as if he were processing her question, didn't speak immediately. "To be honest, I have conflicting emotions about what happened after Annie's graduation and about Annie herself." He took a deep breath, squeezed her hand and then, his voice mellowing, said, "But yes. I will do my darnedest to be here for her."

Geneva closed her eyes, tension draining out of her. She wouldn't live long enough to know the outcome, but somehow she knew this young man would keep his word. "Thank you," she said, patting his hand. "Thank you so much."

Then he had gone back to work. Now, longing for sleep, she wished she had more time, time to see how that gentle, conflicted, lovestruck young man would bring Annie back into the sunlight.

"BUBBA, BUDDY. We're knocking off early today." Kyle unhooked his tool belt and put it in the storage unit in the back of his truck. "Tonight your humble master is supposed to transform himself into Prince Charming and go to the ball."

He opened the cab door and Bubba jumped into the passenger seat, but not before sending Kyle an inquisitive look that clearly communicated, *The hell you say.*

"Yeah, I know." Kyle started up the truck and headed for home. "Not my bag, these country club do's. It's not like I'm duding myself up for my best girl. Nope, pal, I'm going because I'm a damned coward." On the steering wheel, he tapped out time to the song on the radio. "Yep, I had my opportunity the other morning. I should've told Rosemary to forget it."

Why hadn't he? Pure and simple, he hadn't want to hurt Rosemary. She was so nice. If only he could find a reason to be miffed with her or to disapprove of her. But she was every bit as likable as all the Nemecs generally were. And he'd known her for practically her whole life. On paper, they were the perfect match.

It wasn't only Rosemary's expectations that he had to deal with. Bruce and Janet Nemec, Margaret, Rita, his fellow employees, hell, they all assumed the two of them would end up together.

He'd tried, really. But you can't create a spark with wet tinder. He didn't know much about love. Certainly not from his bully of an old man or the mother who had deserted him. In fact, the Nemecs were his main role models for what a marriage ought to look like. And Pete and Annie for what young love should be. Thinking about the two examples, he couldn't envision himself walking into the sunset with Rosemary. At no time had he felt the involuntary surge of passion for her that, despite his efforts to the contrary, he now did for Annie.

He hadn't asked for these feelings. But they were there, and he was having no success getting rid of them. He could grit his teeth, look the other way, steer his thoughts in a different direction—none of it worked.

"Tonight's the night, Bubba. I don't know what this'll do to my position with Bruce, but I have to be honest with Rosemary."

As always, the dog sent him a look confirming his complete support of Kyle's plan.

LATE THAT AFTERNOON clouds gathered on the horizon and wind nipped at the beach, sending little sand devils skittering across the expanse. Then at about four-thirty, a curtain of rain wrapped the cottage in a gray cocoon. A perfect chowder evening, Annie thought, as she chopped potatoes and onion and opened a tin of clams. Geneva had spent most of the afternoon in bed, and the two times Annie had checked on her, she had been sleeping peacefully. The kitchen radio, tuned to a classical station, provided the only sound other than that of rain pattering on the roof and slashing against windowpanes. The darkening day could have been depressing; instead, it enhanced the coziness of their home. They were safe, a good dinner simmered on the stove and they had each other. Annie leaned against the counter, needing desperately to treasure this moment, the comfort and normalcy of it.

Later they ate dinner in the living room, the soft strains of Pachebel's "Canon in D Major" playing in the background. Geneva wore her deep purple fleece robe with crimson slippers. Between sips of soup, Annie studied her and decided the nap had been beneficial. Her face had color and she seemed more animated than usual. Her breaths were labored but steady.

"I love the rain," Geneva said as she set her soup bowl aside and stared out the window. "It's as if God decides to cleanse his world."

"One in dire need of it," Annie commented, her thoughts flying to Afghanistan and Iraq where mortar fire and bombings made life so very tenuous.

"When I was tiny, I used to be afraid of storms. But then one summer night, my father came and woke me. 'I have something to show you,' he said. 'Something miraculous.' He wrapped me in a blanket and carried me out on the porch. A terrific thunder and lightning storm lashed the coast. 'Isn't God a splendid artist? Look there! And there!' And so it went. From that evening on, I was a lover of storms. So exciting." Geneva paused to cough into a tissue. "But this is equally thrilling in a different way. Yes—" she nodded to herself "—cleansing. That's what it is."

Annie nested her bowl inside Geneva's and carried the tray into the kitchen. She would do the dishes later, she decided, in order to take advantage of Geneva's alertness.

In the living room she settled back in her chair. "Do you want to redeem yourself for your gin rummy loss last night?"

Geneva snorted. "Your victory was a fluke, and ordinarily I'd take you on. But I have something else in mind for tonight."

"What?"

Geneva's expression turned somber. "Cleansing."

"I don't know what you're talking about."

"Oh, I think you do. I told you earlier we needed to have a serious talk. Tonight is the night."

The room closed in on Annie.

"I am not going to 'shuffle off this mortal coil,' as Shakespeare put it, before we dig into the past."

A ghostlike chill raised the hair on the back of Annie's neck. She tried to speak, but her throat turned to dust.

"Child of my heart, you are not happy. You live like a spirit caught between this world and the next. The past is an anchor keeping you forever captive. This can't go on."

Finally Annie's voice returned, along with an ache that went clear to the bone. "I can't! Please!" She tried to stand, to escape, but Geneva's firm grip on her hands rooted her to the spot. As if in slow motion, she sank back into the chair, her face a mask. If she didn't listen, if she didn't talk, none of this could hurt her. She folded her arms defensively. She would sit here in silence for as long as it took.

"I can outwait you," Geneva said. "We're going to do this if it takes all night and I exhaust my oxygen supply."

The two stared at each other. Geneva's eyes, so full of love, made it difficult for Annie to maintain her aloofness. Minutes passed. The clock struck seven. Geneva coughed again. *You don't have to say anything. She can't make you.* As if her stomach were an expanding balloon, Annie felt pressure in her chest. The nightmare would never be over. Auntie G. was wrong to think she could change that.

"Were you pregnant?"

Annie's head jerked up. "Pregnant?" *My God, is that what people thought happened?* Her eyes filled with tears. That would have been vastly preferable to the reality. Pete's baby? Fierce longing sent her to the edge of hysteria.

"No," she said.

"Well, then, I didn't think so. Nina would have told me. So…if you weren't pregnant, there's only one other explanation. You were afraid. A girl doesn't just up and run away the morning after her high school graduation, leaving no trace of her whereabouts, unless she's terrified of something." Auntie G. massaged her chest, as if her next utterance caused her great pain. "Or someone."

Annie clenched her fists, fingernails biting into the tender flesh of her palms. *Don't let the words out. Don't go back to that place.*

"Annie." Her great-aunt's tone was peremptory. "I want the truth. Was it Pete?"

She thought she might suffocate, so sharp was the dagger of Geneva's suspicion, her unthinkable suspicion. "Pete? Oh my God, Auntie G. Pete? He was the best thing that ever happened to me, and now, and now…" She couldn't go on, doubled over with the paroxysms of grief racking her thin body. *Pete! Pete!* She didn't know if she was calling for him aloud or in the void of her great need. All she knew was that he wasn't coming to rescue her. Nobody was. Just as nobody had that night. Not even God.

She could taste bile rising up from her stomach and into her throat. She gagged on her tears.

Somewhere in the riot of her emotions, she heard Auntie G.'s voice, numb but dead calm. "So. I always suspected."

Annie waited, knowing she teetered on the brink of the known world, ready to be blasted into chaos. Auntie G. knew.

Then the word came. The single, odious syllable. "George."

Annie barely made it to the bathroom before bile spewed from deep within.

CHAPTER SEVEN

RAIN FELL IN SHEETS, so Kyle dropped Rosemary at the entrance to the country club before parking the car. Dodging puddles, he hurried to join her, but could not avoid getting thoroughly drenched. Stepping into the men's room, he dried his hands and face and slicked back his hair. He stared at his reflection in the mirror, getting a brief glimpse of what a condemned prisoner might look like. There was no way this evening could end well. Sighing, he swiped at his suit jacket, straightened his shoulders and marched toward the Nemec Construction table, where Bruce, Janet, Margaret and her husband, Rick Baird, were in animated conversation with an older couple he didn't recognize. Rosemary sat quietly, hands folded in her lap, watching his approach, a delighted smile on her lips.

When he reached the table, Bruce rose and gestured expansively. "I think you know everyone except perhaps Gene and Phyllis Hart." Kyle nodded perfunctorily in the direction of the silver-haired man and his plump, bejeweled wife. "Gene is one of the investors in Coastview," Bruce said, referring to a condominium development the company was contracted to build.

"Pleased to meet you," Kyle said, extending a hand before taking his seat between Rosemary and Margaret. Rosemary looked up at him. "Hi, you," she whispered softly before reaching out to brush a few remaining raindrops from his shoulder.

Glancing around, he could see that the club was in full charity gala mode. On each table leather-bound volumes were tastefully arranged among bouquets of wildflowers. Candles, set in Williamsburg brass holders, completed the centerpieces. Blow-ups of classic book covers graced the walls. Animated chatter filled the room. When the waiter set an elaborate surf-and-turf plate in front of him, Kyle couldn't help wondering how much a table for eight had set Bruce back.

Throughout dinner, Rosemary chatted about her recent shopping trip to Portland and her decision to get an apartment and move out of her parents' house. Margaret, on the other hand, had barely said two words to him, concentrating instead on socializing with Phyllis Hart. Tucking a finger between his neck and the stiff shirt collar, he longed for a breath of fresh air, for open spaces. Janet politely inquired about his progress on the Greer cottage, a topic he seized on gratefully, rambling on far too long about wood veneers and extraordinary cabinetry.

He never thought he'd say it, but he was relieved when the band struck up their first number. He stood and pulled back Rosemary's chair. "Dance?"

Her eyes fluttered coquettishly. "I'd love to."

She moved gracefully, accommodating herself to his awkwardness. In his ear, she sang the words to each song, and he could swear she put special emphasis on

lyrics containing the word *love*. His collar was strangling him, and for the rest of the evening he moved
automatically between dancing and sitting at the table
enduring topics of conversation that seemed to have
nothing to do with him.

All the while, dread sat like a lead weight in his
stomach. He knew he could no longer play his part in
this charade with Rosemary. He couldn't think what
he'd ever done to encourage her, but the proprietary
way she adjusted his necktie and ordered extra whipped
cream for his sundae signaled ownership loud and clear.
These actions did not go unnoticed by Bruce and Janet.
Their knowing smiles indicated their approval.

Finally at eleven he could stand it no longer. "If you
all will excuse us, Rosemary and I will be taking off."

"So soon?" Margaret's tone was curious.

On the other hand, Janet's voice carried all the delight
of a mother cat observing her kitten's first foray into the
world. "You young people," she said, shaking her head
in mock dismay. "Enjoy yourselves."

Bruce circled the table and clapped a hand on Kyle's
shoulder. "Thanks for coming, son. Be good to that
daughter of mine."

Rosemary tucked her arm through Kyle's and
beamed up at him. "He will, Daddy."

Kyle acknowledged the Harts, then, feeling worse
than he had the whole evening, he escorted Rosemary
to the coat-check counter, where he retrieved her
raincoat. "All set?"

She ran a hand over his jacket front. "You bet," she
said breathily.

It was only when they were in the car that he realized he had no place to take her for the conversation he intended to have. Going to her parents' house was too weird, and he sure as hell couldn't give her any ideas by taking her to his place. The truck? Too confining and intimate. "Feel like some coffee?" he asked in desperation.

She gave him a funny look. "That wasn't exactly what I had in mind."

He forced himself to smile. "I thought that in this stormy weather a cappuccino sounded good."

She shrugged. "Whatever. Your call."

Yes, he decided. A public place would be best. Neutral territory.

After placing their order at the local Starbucks, he led her to a window table, partially shielded by a display rack of specialty ground coffees. "We could have ordered cappuccinos at the club, you know," she murmured.

"I suppose." He knew she wanted him to say something like *But I wanted you all to myself.* He looked over her shoulder, eyeing the pickup counter. "Hey, I think those are ours." On the way to get the coffees and on the way back, the word *coward* thundered in his mind. He put down the drinks and settled back into his seat.

She took a sip of her coffee, then licked the dab of whipped cream from her lips. She sat without saying anything for a while, slowly rotating the cup between her fingers. Finally she looked up. "What's this about, Kyle? You seemed uncomfortable this evening."

"Sorry, I didn't realize it showed."

"Oh, I don't know if anyone else noticed. You went

through the motions just fine. But I had hoped for…"
She stared out the window.

He made the move out of his comfort zone. "What?"

She turned back. "A deeper connection."

"Something more romantic than platonic?"

"If I'm honest, yes. It's embarrassing to tell you this, but I've had a crush on you my whole life. When you and Pete were in high school, I even kept a scrapbook full of clippings and pictures of you. When Pete would write home from Guard camp and then from Afghanistan, I'd always wait for the good parts…the parts about you."

"Rosemary, please—"

"No, let me finish. It was like a dream come true when you returned from Asia and went to work for my dad. I could see you every day. You would notice me, and then, maybe, you would come to care about me…a lot."

Tears pooled in her eyes. Absently she dipped the tip of her forefinger into the whipped cream and slowly licked it off. "I guess it was a foolish fantasy."

"Not so foolish. Rosemary, you are a lovely, attractive young woman who will make somebody very happy one day."

"Just not you, I guess."

The onset of bitterness in her voice was like the scrape of chalk. "This is what I needed to talk to you about and maybe I shouldn't have waited so long. I don't know how these things happen or why they don't. Loving you, marrying you, that would be the Hollywood ending. Pete would've approved, your family would accept me, you would provide the kind of home I've been missing since I was a kid."

"Go ahead. Say it. I'm not the one."

He took a fortifying breath. "No, Rosemary. For many reasons, I wish you were. But you're not. A friend, yes, and I value that friendship. Honestly, though, there's nothing more. I hate hurting you, but I'd hurt you more if I let this go any further."

"Is there...is there someone else?" Her voice quivered.

How could he answer her when he didn't know himself? All he knew was that, against all reason, Annie had the capacity to make him forget all the times he'd cursed her name on Pete's behalf—and his own. "Not yet," he said quietly.

She picked up her cup and stood. "I think we're done here, Kyle. Please take me home."

They drove in silence to the Nemecs' house. When he pulled to a stop in the driveway and shut off the motor, he turned and laid a hand on her shoulder. "If I've misled you, Rosemary, I'm sorry. I think the world of you and wish you only the best. I hope we can continue as friends. After all, we'll be working together."

He heard the stuttering of her inhalation. "I...I need time, Kyle. The death of a dream isn't easy."

Before he could react, she slipped from the truck, ran to the front door and let herself in.

The only sound in the truck was the swish of windshield wipers. The only smell, the lingering fragrance of Rosemary's cloying perfume.

He'd hurt her. For that, he was truly sorry. Rosemary deserved better. She deserved a man who would love her wholeheartedly. And that man, Kyle knew, would never be him.

ANNIE DIDN'T KNOW how long she'd been sitting on the tile floor, clutching the cool porcelain of the commode, her skin chilled with prickles of fear, the sour taste of memory befouling her mouth. Her hair hung in hanks. When she tucked a handful behind her ear, her fingers brushed her cheek, flushed from the upheaval of her stomach.

As if from a great distance, she heard the squeak of Auntie G.'s walker rumbling toward her. When she looked up, eyes blurring with tears, her great-aunt stood behind her wringing out a washcloth that she then placed on the back of Annie's neck beneath her hair. For a moment there was icy shock, then the relief of sub-siding nausea.

For a long moment neither of them spoke, only the drip of the lavatory faucet punctuating the silence. Auntie G.'s hand, cool and dry, caressed Annie's forehead in wordless comfort.

Slowly Annie raised her head, puzzled. Something was missing. What? The thread of the question pulled her back into the moment. It was too quiet. Then it came to her and she struggled to her knees. "Your oxygen. Auntie G., your oxygen. Where is it?"

"Shh. I'm all right. It's in the other room."

"But…why…?"

"I wanted to move fast. That blasted thing slows me down." She took a couple of labored breaths. "I needed to get to you."

Levering herself up, Annie stood shakily on trem-bling legs. "I'm sorry. So sorry."

The next thing she knew, she was in Auntie G.'s arms, her head buried in the softness of the old woman's fleece

robe, the familiar, faint scent of lavender the sweetest
smell in the world. For a fleeting second, Annie felt safe.

"My darling girl, I had no idea it was so bad. I wish
you had told me then. Maybe I could've helped."

Annie allowed herself to pause, resting against her
great-aunt's shoulder, wishing she could remain there
forever. When she finally stepped back, her eyes locked
on Auntie G.'s. "No. Nobody could help."

In the harsh light of the bathroom, Auntie G.'s face
was ashen, her eyes tortured. "We've started," she said.
"Let's finish this tonight." She turned and began wheel-
ing herself down the hall.

Finish? Annie clutched her stomach. It would never
be finished. Not now. Not ever. But she owed her great-
aunt an explanation. Owed her the words she had never
shared, words that would come from a subterranean
place barricaded by years of shame and silence. Trailing
her aunt back to the living room, Annie prayed for
strength to the God that had once, on a long-ago night,
abandoned her.

"I HAVE A BETTER IDEA," Geneva said as she reinserted
the oxygen tube once she reached the living room.
"Let's get some extra pillows and pile into my bed with
a cup of tea. Far cozier, don't you think?"

Annie nodded. "Chamomile or blackberry?"

"Blackberry."

Annie helped her back to the bedroom before she left
to prepare the tea. Just as well. Geneva needed time to
think. Her immediate reaction had been rage. Rage at
whatever fate had left Annie defenseless against her step-

father. Rage at herself for being halfway around the earth. But her anger would change nothing. She needed to focus on tonight. That's all she had. And maybe a few more short weeks. She needed to marshal every last bit of her strength, wisdom and sensitivity for the task ahead.

Annie, her face mottled and pale, returned soon enough with the bed tray, on which were a teapot, creamer and sugar and two cups and saucers. She had pulled on an oversize fisherman's sweater and, after setting the tray on Geneva's lap, clambered to the other side of the bed, where she sat, knees drawn up, nursing her tea.

"Where would you like to start, pumpkin?"

Annie screwed up her face. "You know, from the beginning, I thought he loved me. Really loved me."

"George?"

"Yes. Mother was so happy with her big house, her designer clothes, her country club membership. At last she had a man who could give her the things we never had after my father died in the accident. She wanted me to have more, too—dance lessons, summer camps...everything." She held the cup to her nose, inhaling, then sipping. "George never denied me anything. And I was so excited to have a new daddy. I thought he was the handsomest man I'd ever seen.

"When I was younger, he'd ask me to sit on his lap. He'd play with my hair. Call me pet names. Cream puff. Princess." She choked on the last word. "When I was older, I'd feel his eyes on me and blush when he told me how pretty I was. I was starved for a father's love and approval. Gradually, though, something about the way he stared at me began to make me uncomfortable. I didn't know why. Not then."

"What about your mother?"

"She was thrilled that George and I got along so well. She kept saying that he loved me like a daughter and didn't I appreciate all he'd done for the two of us. Besides, there was nothing overt that I could point to. So…it was easier to try to ignore him. I even managed…for quite a while."

Geneva clamped her lips shut in the effort not to lash out at Liz, long dead but no less culpable. "Did you say anything to anyone else?"

Annie set down her cup and drew a shuddering sigh. "No."

Geneva put her arm around Annie and cuddled her back against the pillows. "Tell me about your Pete."

"Oh, Auntie G., it's so hard to talk about him." She blinked rapidly and swiped a wrist under her nose. "I loved him so."

"There, there. Take your time."

"He was the love of my life." A dirge could not have sounded more mournful. "Sometimes I still can't believe he's gone. We met sophomore year. In geometry class. He sat across the aisle, one row in front of me. I couldn't keep my eyes off him. He had thick black hair and beautiful brown eyes that were so full of life and humor. And he was smart, too. He was studying theorems and me? Well, I was studying him. I thought he'd never notice me. I mean, he was a football player, even made varsity that year. Just looking at him, I'd forget what I was about to say."

"Then one day he noticed you?"

She nestled against Geneva, her fingers curled into the fleece of her robe. "One day...the best day. He followed me out of class to my locker. He leaned against the door so that I couldn't open it. 'What's the password?' he said. Password? I didn't know what he was talking about. I asked him what he meant. 'A yes will do.' He gazed at me with those dreamy eyes of his and I'd have said yes to anything. 'Will you go to the Homecoming dance with me?'" She rolled over and sat up, once more hugging her knees. "We were inseparable from that day on. I spent a lot of time at the Nemecs' house. They were such a special family. On some level I think I knew that what they shared was more genuine than what I had with Mother and George."

"Things at home must have changed after your mother died." Geneva winced inwardly. Liz's funeral. Another time she'd been halfway around the world. She waited, wondering what images were playing through her great-niece's mind.

"At first, I was numb. Her death felt unreal to me. One day I went into her room, you know, just to try to feel her presence, smell her smells. Everything was gone. Without telling me, the housekeeper had packed up her things and given them to charity. George's orders, she said. That's when I got angry. I screamed at her, at George, at my mother for leaving me, at the fact I was helpless and alone. I stayed up in my bedroom and refused to come out for several days. The only person I wanted with me was Pete. He brought me a bouquet of daisies and simply sat with me, saying little, just holding my hand. I cried as I never had before, and he seemed to know to let me sob to my heart's content. When I finally stopped and could breathe again, he cupped my face in his warm hands and he looked deep into my eyes. He said, 'I love you, Annie. I always will. I promise to take care of you, no matter what.'" She turned to Geneva. "And he always did. All but once."

The overwhelming sadness in Annie's voice was pitiful. It was that "once" that had transformed a bright, lovely young woman into a shell of her former self. "What happened that Pete couldn't keep his promise?"

Annie drained her teacup, but continued holding it as if clinging to its warmth. "It wasn't Pete. I knew I could count on him. It was me."

"What do you mean?"

"I didn't want Pete involved."

The story was Annie's to tell. Geneva knew her role was limited to gentle prodding. "When…?"

Setting down the cup, Annie raked both hands through her hair, then turned to her great-aunt, her voice brittle. "George raped me."

Even though Geneva had been anticipating the words, the sound of them uttered aloud cracked her in two. She reached out to Annie, who sat rigid, lost in her own hell, her hazel eyes expressionless. Impotent, Geneva let her hands drop to her lap, searching desperately for the right thing to say. But there could be no "right" words because nothing would ever change the hideous reality.

"Graduation night. Afterward," Annie said tonelessly. She shifted her position, as if winding up the motor of her memory. "During my senior year, George kept

watching me. One time when I came home from swim-
ming, he tried to hide it with a newspaper, but I could
see he had an erection. I tried to rationalize that it was
something he was reading that caused it."

Geneva groaned.

"He'd make these comments about how nice it was
now that it was just the two of us and how we needed
to get closer since we were each other's only family. All
the time he was telling me how beautiful I was, how
'foxy.' I hated that word and hated how it made me feel.
Soiled. Toward spring when he kept talking about how
I could make my own decisions when I turned eighteen
in May, I got really scared, but I never thought he'd do
what he did. I planned to leave home before anything
happened. But then sometimes I wondered if I was
imagining it all. Or if in some way I was doing something to encourage him."

Geneva interrupted. "Annie, no. None of it was your
fault. Don't think that for one minute."

Annie smiled sadly, then continued. "Anyway, I deliberately started wearing baggy clothes and avoided
him whenever I could. But then he started coming into
my room to say good-night, sitting on the bed, rubbing
his hand up and down my arm. I'd close my eyes
because I couldn't bear the sort of breathless way he
looked at me."

"Child, you must have been terrified."

"I kept thinking that I could outlast him. After
graduation, I would go off to summer school at the university and never come back."

"So...you told Pete?"

"Only that something about George made me feel weird. Pete knew me well enough to know something was wrong. One night in the spring, I was taking a shower. Getting ready for a date. George walked into the bathroom, and when I turned around, there he was. Just staring at me. I had no idea how long he'd been there. It freaked me out. That night Pete saw that I was upset. He kept asking me why. So I told him."

"And?"

"He listened to the whole story. Then he took me by the arms and stared at me. 'So help me God,' he said, 'if that son of a bitch lays one hand on you, I'll kill him. I promise.' Pete was intense, and I believed him. He knew all about guns. You know how you can tell when somebody's telling the truth? So if I had ever let on that George raped me, Pete wouldn't have wasted a minute thinking about the consequences. I truly believe he would have shot George in cold blood." She snugged her hands up into the sleeve of her sweater. "I couldn't let that happen. So I left. Before Pete could kill him."

She squeezed her eyes tight for a moment before going on. "And before I did something I'd regret. I felt so violated and angry, I might have murdered him myself if I'd had the means. All I could do was run. I had no options. I had to get away from George, and I had to keep Pete from ruining his life. He and Kyle were leaving two days after graduation for National Guard training. They'd both always wanted to serve in the military. I figured no one would ever have to know about the rape. Early that next morning, I cleaned myself up and went to the bank first thing to cash my graduation gift checks. Then I called you. I was on the bus to Arizona before anyone realized I was gone."

"But Pete?"

"He and Kyle were leaving early the following morning. I stuck a note on the window of Pete's car. Said I was breaking up with him. He never knew where I went."

"Never? Didn't you write him later?"

"I didn't want anyone to know where I was. I couldn't run the risk of George finding me. Or of Pete going AWOL."

"So that's why you never came back to Eden Bay?"

"When George finally died, I could have, I suppose." She was silent for several minutes. "By then, though, Pete was gone. Killed in Afghanistan. There was nothing here for me anymore. Not a single thing."

The sound of the oxygen machine intruded on Geneva's thoughts, providing a powerful reminder of Annie's sacrifice in returning to care for her. "It must've been extraordinarily difficult for you to come here to be with me."

"It was. But it was something I had to do."

Only then did Annie relax, nestling close. She laid her head on Geneva's shoulder and they stayed that way for a long time without speaking. Geneva caressed Annie's arm, wishing with all her heart that she could turn back time, reverse the results of that night and restore innocence to her precious great-niece.

Somehow Annie needed to move beyond the crippling effects of a damaged past. *But I will not be here to help her.* A wrenching sigh tore from Geneva's lungs. In the dark of this night, with wind and rain lashing the

house, there had to be a ray of hope, something or
someone to cling to.

Was it too much to ask of the young man who had
been Pete Nemec's best friend?

KYLE STRIPPED OFF his tie, hung up his suit, tossed the
dress shirt into the laundry basket and strolled in his
skivvies to the refrigerator. He reached for the lone beer
on the shelf, popped the top and took a long draft.
Walking to the front window, he looked out at the rain-
water coursing down the street and trees battered by the
wind. Finally he turned away and sank onto the sofa,
hardly aware that Bubba had joined him. This evening
had been a disaster, and Monday, when he had to face
the Nemecs again, would be even worse. It was as if an
unknown hand had taken a nearly completed jigsaw
puzzle of his life and dumped the pieces on the floor.
He didn't know where he stood with anyone.

Had the Nemecs shared Rosemary's expectations?
Margaret had always been the protective big sister, both
of Pete and Rosemary. After tonight, she'd probably
never speak to him again. Ever since he was a kid, Bruce
and Janet had been more parents to him than his own.
And how was he repaying them? He drained the beer.
By rejecting their daughter, that's how.

Bubba nuzzled Kyle's chest, then laid his head in his
lap. No matter what Kyle's sins, the dog remained faithful, affectionate. But he couldn't expect that of people,
people whom he'd hurt and betrayed. Next week would
be pure hell. Would he even still have a job?

He laid back his head. Could he have done anything

differently? Played along until Rosemary could see they had no future together? Hell, he'd known the answer to that one before he even formed the question.

Would anything have changed if Annie hadn't come back to Eden Bay? He sighed. Certainly not as it concerned Rosemary. Was anything really different now?

He wanted to say no, but he couldn't. Not when Annie's name caught in his throat and caused him six degrees of discomfort. Restless, he stood up, dislodging Bubba, and crushed the beer can in his hand. Damn it. He'd broken Rosemary's heart and now was coveting Pete's girl. None of it made any sense. He'd spent ten years cursing Annie, furious over her cavalier treatment of his friend.

Bubba tugged at the hem of his boxers, as if to urge him to bed. Kyle resisted. He was exhausted, but no way was he going to lie there in the dark waiting for the nightmare to come, as he knew it would. Especially tonight.

Because there was one more sin he had rarely admitted, even to himself…something he'd tried to suppress ever since high school. The long and the short of it was this. He had been in love with Annie from the first time he'd seen her.

All he could do at the time was stand by and watch helplessly as Pete lost his heart to Annie and she to him. And do his damnedest to be their friend. But friendship was tough duty when he wanted so much more and spent sleepless nights dreaming of the girl he couldn't have.

And then in one lonely, desperate moment on that beach, he'd let down his guard and embraced Annie— and felt guilty ever since. Had Pete known? He hoped to God not.

Tossing the beer can in the trash, he resumed his post by the front window, watching a storm that was insignificant compared to his own emotional turmoil. When Annie left town and disappeared abruptly, devastating Pete, it had been all too easy for Kyle to channel his deep feelings into outrage. Outrage that had increased in intensity after the one glance at her photograph that had cost Pete his life.

Who had Kyle been kidding? He'd never forgotten that girl with the warm eyes and dazzling smile. Annie, who made his heart burn in his chest. And…he'd never forgiven her.

Could he now?

Bubba nosed Kyle's leg and looked up with pleading eyes. "Go on to bed, buddy. I can't sleep." Instead the dog hopped onto the sofa and curled into a ball.

Kyle turned off the lights and sat in the darkness questioning everything, especially the fact that he loved a woman who had turned her back on his best friend with no explanation. How could he put his trust in her? Everyone he'd ever loved had abandoned him. Why should she treat him any differently?

CHAPTER EIGHT

WHEN ANNIE FIRST BECAME aware of the shafts of sunlight assaulting her closed eyes, she stirred. Her head felt like a bowling ball—thick and heavy; her mouth, sour. The sharp crick in her neck finally brought her to a sitting position. Beside her, Auntie G. lay on her back, snoring shallowly. Annie massaged the nape of her neck, the reality slowly dawning on her. She'd spent the night in her great-aunt's bed. Then, with the suddenness of a lightning bolt, she remembered why. And felt sick all over again.

She hung her head, once again reliving the shame of her violation, the heartbreak of leaving Pete. It was a Pandora's box she had hoped never to open, even as she had understood all along that one day she might be compelled to. Auntie G. had let her talk, rambling here and there through the ghosts of the past. Yet even so, Annie knew with a terrible realization that last night she had barely tapped the surface. She'd shared nothing of the bereavement she'd endured when Pete had been lost to her that morning after graduation. Nor of the burden of wondering if she'd done something to bring the rape on herself, just as she must have unknowingly done something to encourage Kyle to hug her that evening at the end of their senior year. And certainly nothing of her ongoing fear of being touched in any kind of sexual way.

That was one more reason she needed to keep her distance from Kyle. So far he'd only comforted her, but she couldn't allow herself be lulled by her need for soothing. Maybe she was overreacting or misreading the signals. All she knew was that her own body deceived her when she was around him. And that wasn't fair to him, not when the mere thought of anything more intimate turned her blood to ice water.

With a shake of her head, which did nothing but send BB's cavorting inside her skull, she scooted to the end of the bed and stood up. The thought came to her that an emotional hangover was every bit as debilitating as a liquor-induced one.

Gingerly, she made her way to the kitchen to put on the coffee, then indulged in a long, hot shower, which made her feel minimally better. After throwing on a pair of faded jeans and a baggy Arizona Diamondbacks T-shirt, she went downstairs and poured a cup of coffee. The jolt of heat and caffeine helped restore minimal function to her brain. Cradling the mug in her hand, she tiptoed to Geneva's bedroom door. Her great-aunt's wrinkled, blue-veined hands rested on her chest, which rose and fell sporadically. Her puffy eyes and pale complexion gave her a wasted look. Guiltily Annie reviewed the evening's conversation. What toll had her unburdening taken on Geneva's limited reserves of strength?

Deciding to let her sleep for as long as she needed, Annie ate a bagel smeared with cream cheese and then set about cleaning the house in preparation for Carmen's return Sunday evening. Sadness welled in her heart as Annie reflected on how difficult Geneva's imminent death would be for Carmen as well as for herself. No matter what the personal consequences, Annie was grateful to Carmen for summoning her back to Eden Bay and for the blessing of spending these last precious weeks with Auntie G.

Bent over the counter, a soapy sponge in her hand, Annie crumpled. She couldn't imagine a world without Geneva Greer. Who would ever come to her rescue now? Love her unconditionally?

FROM HIS FIRST LOOK at Rita on Monday morning, Kyle knew the day was headed south. The receptionist greeted Bubba with her customary warmth, but when she turned to Kyle, her lifted eyebrow and sad shake of the head let him know that he, not Bubba, was the one in the doghouse. "Way to go, Romeo," she muttered as he passed her on his way to his cubicle. A quick glance in the direction of Rosemary's empty office gave him some relief. At least he wouldn't have to run into her yet. He figured he'd be doing the walking-on-eggshells dance around the office for quite a while. Although he was worried about the females, it was Bruce's reaction that most concerned him. No father enjoyed seeing his daughter get hurt, even if it was for the best in the long run. Was it a serious enough situation that Kyle's job was in jeopardy? Only time would tell.

Things went from bad to worse when he reached his desk. There lay a phone memo in Rita's unmistakable printing. "Call Margaret immediately." He groaned aloud. A typical firstborn, Margaret had always been protective of Pete and Rosemary. Often that protection came across as controlling. He crumpled the piece of paper and tossed it toward the wastebasket, missing completely. Damn. Was this the day from hell, or what?

Checking the work schedule, he saw that he had to meet a home owner about a bedroom addition, check on a crew laying tile and finish staining some window trim at the Greer cottage. If he talked to Margaret now, his obligations would give him a reason to cut short their conversation. Might as well get it over with.

But when he phoned her, Margaret had other ideas. She insisted he come by her house. *Bite the bullet,* he told himself. Bubba trailed him out of the building and sat quietly on the passenger seat, as if fearful of invading his master's space, which, indeed, was heavy with self-loathing and irritation.

ONE LOOK AT MARGARET and Kyle knew he didn't want to be here. Coolly polite, she ushered him into the living room and indicated he should take a seat on the sofa. "I just fixed some coffee. You take yours black, right?"

"Yes, but I can't stay long." He glanced at his watch. "I have a nine-o'clock appointment."

"Fine," she said. "I'll be right back with the coffee."

While she was in the kitchen, Kyle glanced around the neat, comfortably furnished room. Then he noticed the photographs on the end table. Pete's graduation picture, a family photo with Pete proudly wearing his National Guard uniform and one of Margaret and Pete hugging and clowning for the camera. A sort of mini-shrine, he thought sadly, willing himself to look away.

Entering the room, Margaret handed him a coffee mug. "Here," she said, then perched on an overstuffed chair, balancing her cup on her knees.

"Let's cut to the chase," Kyle began. "What's on your mind?"

"My sister. How could you hurt her like that? You have to have known she's had a crush on you for years. Yesterday we went for a long walk on the beach and all she could talk about was what happened Friday night after the two of you left the club. She's too trusting, but surely you're not so dense that you didn't pick up on her feelings. Leading her on the way you did—"

"Just a minute." Kyle set his coffee on the end of the table. "I never led Rosemary on. I have too much respect for her ever to do that."

"You could've fooled her. And me, for that matter."

Sarcasm didn't become her, but he had to respond. "I have always been fond of Rosemary and have tried not to give her any false hopes. You know, there's the fine line I'm walking here. I have great affection for your entire family. Hell, Pete was the best friend a guy could have. And your folks have always made me feel welcome in their home. But I never suggested to Rosemary that I felt more strongly about her than about the rest of you."

"Well, you must've done something. She practically had the wedding dress picked out. You can't have been so totally oblivious." She stood, hands fisted by her sides. "I don't get it, Kyle. How could you repay all my family's done for you by punting Rosemary? My father gave you a job and this is—"

"You've gone far enough, Margaret." Kyle, too, rose to his feet, barely containing the anger coursing through him. "There never was a good way for this conversation to end. Obviously, there's little I can say that will change your mind about me. But get this. Never, in word or action, did I encourage Rosemary to think we had a future, and I certainly would never have used her as a means of advancing my career with Nemec Construction." He moved toward the door, eager to escape her glare. "You can take my explanation or leave it, but if you think I would ever deliberately hurt anyone in Pete's family, then you don't know me very well."

At the mention of Pete, indignation seemed to drain out of Margaret, and Kyle could see she was close to tears. He found himself softening toward her. On some level, she was entitled. He'd failed Pete once, and now in his sister's book, he'd failed Rosemary.

"I just love her so much," Margaret said.

"I know," he said, moving to the door.

"There's one more thing." He turned, sensing the steel returning to her voice. "Rosemary thinks you've found someone else."

He stared at her. "And if I have? Am I so indebted to the Nemecs that I can't have a life?"

"No, Kyle, by all means suit yourself." Margaret shook her head as if chiding a misbehaving child. "Just don't expect me to be happy for you."

With his hand on the doorknob, he hesitated, choosing his words carefully. "I care about you, Rosemary and your whole family. I hope the time will come when we can move beyond this conversation today." Then he quietly left the house, wondering how he could have made such a mess of things and what repercussions would follow when the Nemecs learned that it was Annie who was increasingly becoming his "someone else."

IT WAS LATE AFTERNOON Monday before Geneva felt like moving from her bed to the wheelchair. Carmen had been hovering over her ever since her arrival the night before, pampering her with a hearty chicken-tortilla soup, sopaipillas and, best of all, her creamy, homemade flan. Even so, Geneva had trouble summoning any appetite.

"Your strength, *señorita*. Please to eat some more."

In Carmen's sad eyes and her own exhausted body, Geneva read the truth. She was much weaker. The simple act of breathing required enormous effort. Now, sitting in the ocean-view bay window, a pillow propped behind her back, she summoned the will to think about the future. The house was in order, or would be when Kyle Becker finished staining the trim. Her legal affairs had been attended to. More troubling was what to do about Annie. Nothing would change the past. The best she could hope for was that Kyle would help Annie through the next few months.

Friday night had been difficult for both of them—and emotionally it had taken more out of her than even she had supposed. Should she have confronted the girl earlier? Somehow helped her to get into counseling? *Hindsight is wonderful,* Geneva thought with a snort.

Drained of the energy to continue their conversation, Geneva had spent the day resting, drifting in and out of sleep. Even now, with sunlight frosting the waves, it was difficult to stay focused either on the scene before her or on her thoughts. Was this how it was? Dying? A gradual fading away. A dimming of the light. Fatigue weighing like a heavy blanket.

"Miss Greer, would you like to see the final results?" How long had Kyle Becker been standing there? Had she fallen asleep again?

"Mercy, you startled me."

"I'm sorry. I didn't mean to."

She waved her hand in dismissal. "No, I know you didn't. And, yes, I would love to see what you've done with the house."

He picked up the oxygen tank and wheeled her slowly through the downstairs, pointing out the floorboards he'd replaced, the newly painted replacement Sheetrock, the refinished mantelpiece and the caulking around the windows. "Now for the upstairs."

"Oh, I can't do that. The wheelchair is heavy and—"

"Nonsense." Then as if he'd done it all his life, Kyle leaned over, put one arm around her shoulders and another under her knees and lifted her, oxygen tank and all. Then, slowly and with great care, he carried her upstairs.

Her eyes filled with tears. She had thought never again see the bedroom in which she'd spent such happy girlhood hours or to catch a glimpse of the panoramic seascape out the upstairs hall dormer window. With his elbow, Kyle rapped on Annie's closed door.

The look on her face when she opened it was priceless—a combination of surprise, doubt and joy. "Auntie G.—"

"We're having a building inspection," Kyle said as he stepped into the room and lowered her to the rocking chair her own mother had used when Geneva had been a little girl.

Glancing around the room and up at the ceiling, she could see that Kyle had repaired the ceiling and refreshed the paint. Her eyes strayed to the double bed and to the quilt her grandmother had made and to the worktable where scraps of material lay in colorful profusion. She drew a deep, labored breath, and whether it was a result of memory or a newly restored sense of smell, the fragrances of lemon oil, salt spray and lavender drifted over her.

"Okay?" Kyle asked.

"Better than that. You've done exactly what I asked. You've restored my past." She reached up and took the young man's hands in hers. "Thank you," she said, looking directly into his eyes. "For everything."

He nodded in understanding, holding the connection for a beat. That was when she became convinced. He would be there for Annie.

They continued the eye contact until Annie spoke up. "We were lucky, weren't we, Auntie G., to find such a fine craftsman."

Geneva smiled. "And such a fine human being." Before sentiment took an even greater toll, she turned to Annie and nodded toward the worktable. "Now that I'm up here, show me some more of your creations."

Kyle waited while Annie spread out an array of

purses, beautifully made and wildly distinctive. In her day, Geneva knew, she would not have hesitated to spend a small fortune for one.

The clatter of footsteps on the stairs interrupted the inspection. *"Santo Dios! Señorita."* Carmen stood panting in the doorway. "I was worried. You disappear. I look and look."

"I'm sorry," Kyle said. "I should have told you I brought Miss Greer up here."

"Please, young man, call me Auntie G."

Kyle placed a hand on her shoulder. "I'd be honored." Then he added in a raspy voice, "Auntie G."

Geneva glanced from her beloved great-niece to Carmen, her faithful friend, and then to the strong young man to whom she had committed her dear Annie. "I love you all," she said simply. "But I'm tired. Kyle, could you—"

"My pleasure, Auntie G." Then, as if she were light as a feather, he cradled her in his arms and started down the stairs.

It felt so good to surrender to his strength, to let herself be carried against his warm chest and rest in the steady beat of his heart. In that moment, she knew it with overpowering relief. All would be well. She could go now.

EARLY THURSDAY AFTERNOON Annie perched on a kitchen stool chopping onions for the casserole Carmen was preparing. As the older woman worked, she hummed a sweetly mournful tune under her breath. The shared quiet, while companionable, was also fraught with the unutterable. Each day since Auntie G.'s trip upstairs, she had grown frailer, her breathing more erratic and difficult, her wakeful periods shorter. On Tuesday Annie had called the doctor and the social worker, making arrangements for full nursing care, beginning Sunday when Carmen was to leave. So long as Carmen was here, comforting in her concern and efficiency, Annie could cope. But with strangers under the roof? She didn't know how she could bear it. She sniffled, lying to herself that the onions were responsible for the moisture clouding her eyes.

"Is soon, *mi niña*."

Annie didn't pretend to misunderstand. "I know."

"I pray for peaceful end. Your *tia*, she had a good life. Sunshine, friends, love, beauty. And you."

Setting down the knife, Annie pulled a tissue from her pocket and blew her nose. "Thank you, Carmen. I like hearing about how happy she was. She makes other people happy, too, just being around her. Like Kyle Becker."

Where had that come from? She had stored Monday's bittersweet memory of Kyle showing Auntie G. the house, afraid to draw it out and examine it too closely. Because in the moment when he'd picked up the old woman and held her close, Annie had fallen in love with him. When had that playful, teasing guy she'd known in high school turned into a kind and gentle man who knew intuitively what her great-aunt needed?

"Señor Kyle, he made this home a palace for her."

"And for me." Then, out of the blue, Annie was struck by what would happen next. After…after… She wouldn't let her mind form the words. Would she be able to stay here? Or was it time to go in a different direction? But could she bring herself to sell the family cottage? A feeling of rudderlessness swept over her, matched only by that May morning when she'd fled Eden Bay and all that was familiar. Now, paradoxically, it was that very familiarity that confused her. In subtle ways with each passing day, she was feeling more at home here, even with all its difficult memories, than she did in Bisbee.

Carmen resumed her humming. Annie slid from the stool and went to check on her great-aunt. Tiptoeing into the darkened room, she inspected the oxygen level in the tank. Fine, for now. Then she stood at the end of the bed, trying to memorize each detail of Auntie G.'s face. Yet this was not the face she wanted to remember. She turned to the bureau and studied the framed photograph of a younger Auntie G. sitting at a Parisian outdoor café, her short dark hair curling around her face, her delighted smile welcoming someone off camera. One of her lovers? It was this vibrant creature Annie could remember swooping into town once in a blue moon, bringing with her the most exotic gifts from places with strange-sounding names—Istanbul, Kuala Lumpur, Nairobi. No matter the occasion or how much time had elapsed since Annie had seen her, Auntie G. always had a knack for making her feel special.

She didn't know how long she'd stood there, as if by doing so she could stave off the inevitable, when the phone ringing in the kitchen drew her attention. Reluctantly, she left the bedside.

"For you." Carmen met her in the hall, handing her the portable phone.

"Annie, it's Carolee. I was wondering about your aunt."

As she filled Carolee in on Geneva's condition, Annie walked toward the stairs and sat on the third step, clinging to this sympathetic voice from the outside world.

"It sounds as if you're doing all the right things. I'm glad you're having home care. Those nurses are great and will be a big help. Besides, my friend, you need to tend to yourself. It's pretty easy for the caregiver to get run-down."

"I appreciate your call, Carolee. I needed a reality check. It's easy to lose track of the days."

"Understandable. I, uh, have another reason for calling. I thought maybe you could use a change of scene. If I came by later this afternoon, would you be able to join me for a walk on the beach? So often when I get home from my shift at the hospital, there's so much to do that my exercise routine suffers, as you could undoubtedly tell from my, shall we say, ample body. Anyway, I'd love your company."

Carolee's unpretentious chatter provided a sorely needed tonic. "I think I could leave Auntie G. for a while and, frankly, right about now a walk on the beach sounds better that a full-blown spa treatment."

They settled on a time, and when Annie returned the phone to its cradle, her mood had lightened.

KYLE HAD SUCCESSFULLY avoided coming into contact with Rosemary for the better part of the week. With time, he supposed, their relationship would become less awkward. Particularly if Margaret would stop fueling the fire. Bruce had been in and out of the office, preoccupied with getting municipal approval for the condominium development. Likewise, Kyle himself had been mostly out of the office the past few days, so there had been no time to talk with Bruce. Delaying the inevitable conversation wasn't an option. Kyle needed to find out where he stood.

He'd stayed late on this Thursday to work up a bid on a huge home renovation, one where the new owner had said, "Spare no expense." If he could pull it off, the project would be a showcase for AAA Builders. Before last Friday night with Rosemary, it might even have been a stepping stone toward eventually taking over when Bruce retired.

Rita and the office staff had left for the day when he heard the front door open. Stepping into the lobby, Bruce was balancing rolled-up sets of plans. "Here, let me help." Kyle stepped forward and relieved the man of his burden, and then followed him into his darkened office where he set the plans on a conference table. "How'd it go with the planning commission?"

Bruce turned on the desk lamp and sank into his leather desk chair. "As usual, we hit a few snags, but I'm hopeful it's something that can be addressed." He let out a sigh. "Construction I enjoy. Red tape is another matter." Then, as if remembering his manners, he looked up and said, "Have a seat."

Bruce filled him in on the problems with the condo project and they brainstormed possible solutions. When they'd exhausted the subject, the worry lines had eased around Bruce's eyes. "Thanks, Kyle. I appreciate those suggestions."

Kyle felt his stomach muscles tighten. "If you have the time, there's something I'd like to discuss with you."

"Janet's off at bridge club, so I have nothing but time. Shoot."

"This is a ticklish subject, one I'm not real comfortable with."

Bruce leaned forward, clasping his hands on his desk. "You can talk to me about anything, son."

"It's Rosemary."

The older man nodded. "I thought so. You won't be surprised to learn the Nemec females are pretty upset."

"I figured as much. What about you?" Kyle felt perspiration gathering between his shoulder blades. "Your opinion matters a lot to me. I want you to know that I never intended to hurt Rosemary. That would be disrespectful to you and would dishonor Pete."

"Let's get one thing straight. Your personal life and the business are two separate things. If you're worried about your job, let me set your mind at ease. You're too valuable to me and to the company to let something like a failed romance stand in the way."

Kyle's grip on the chair relaxed. "I appreciate that."

Bruce cocked an eyebrow. "You were never in love with her." It wasn't a question.

"I think the world of Rosemary. She's been like a kid sister. But love? No."

"She has a romantic streak. I've been wondering if fixating on you wasn't one way she tried to hold her brother close."

Kyle couldn't overlook the sadness coloring the man's eyes. "Maybe. I imagine we all try to do that. There isn't a day that I don't think of Pete."

"She'll get over her disappointment. Sure, I don't like seeing her upset, but she deserves to be loved."

"I couldn't agree more. In some ways, I wish it could've been me. Your family means so much."

"And that isn't going away. We'll ride out this storm. All of us. I love my daughter. However, I suspect any heartbreak is more due to her wishful thinking than to any fault of yours." He stood and extended his hand. "Thanks for clearing the air, son."

In that moment, the man's fairness and affection reminded Kyle so much of Pete that he found it difficult to speak. All he could do was nod before retreating to his cubicle.

ANNIE WAITED for Carolee on the porch, enjoying, as best she could, the mild spring evening. When Carolee pulled up in an older-model Toyota and parked, Annie noticed she was still wearing her pink scrubs. "I didn't have time to change," Carolee said, approaching the porch. Her flyaway hair blew in the wind and Annie could see a hint of the girl she used to know beneath the matronly exterior.

Smiling, Annie stood. "I wasn't aware there was a beach dress code."

Carolee returned the smile. "Well, thank God for that. Ready?"

"I've been looking forward to it. Let's go."

On their way down to the beach, Carolee asked more

questions about Geneva, and Annie shared her concern about her great-aunt's weakening condition.

"That's often the way it is with congestive heart failure," Carolee said sympathetically. "At some point breathing puts too much stress on the heart. It must be difficult to stand by, feeling helpless."

Carolee's understanding moved Annie deeply, and for a few moments they walked in silence. Matching each other stride for stride, they'd gone about half a mile down the beach when Carolee spoke.

"What are your plans? Will you stay in Eden Bay?"

Annie appreciated that Carolee had not added *after your great-aunt's death*.

"I-I'm not sure." It had been one thing to ponder this question for herself, but to be confronted with it by another brought her uncertain future front and center.

"You always seemed so happy here." Carolee stopped, studying the waves crashing along the shoreline. Then she faced Annie. "What happened to that happiness?"

"Happiness is sometimes in the eye of the beholder. My life was not always what it seemed to others."

"It must've been hard for you after your mother died."

"Yes, it was." Annie started walking, familiar dread spreading through her. She would never again be ready to talk about George.

"You might be surprised how many friends you have here."

Two that I can count. Carolee and Kyle. "I left, Carolee. Abruptly. Without any explanation. I imagine that's hard for some to forget. There are bound to be questions, and I'm not strong enough to face them."

"Nobody's asking, Annie. At least I'm not. Whatever happened that caused you to leave happened in the past. This is now." She linked her arm through Annie's. "I'd love it if you stayed. I could use a friend like you."

The invitation spread a warm glow through Annie's body. To be wanted in Eden Bay. Accepted with no strings. It was a heady prospect. "Thank you, Carolee. I appreciate your friendship. Especially right now."

At the breakwater, they turned and reversed their steps. Heading up the hill toward the cottage, Carolee drew ragged breaths. Bending over and placing her hands on her knees, she rested momentarily. "See how out of shape I am? Gotta make myself do this more often."

"Anytime. I'd enjoy your company."

Carolee straightened. "Me, too, Annie. Me, too."

They had made it to Carolee's car when Carmen burst out the door and ran to the edge of the porch. "Annie, please to come quickly." Above the wind, her next words made Annie momentarily dizzy. "It's *Señorita.*"

Carolee sprinted with her to the house where they followed Carmen into the bedroom. Geneva's face was waxen and her breaths came in shuddering rales. Carolee quickly examined her, then drew Annie into the hall.

"Honey, you have a choice here. My experience tells me she won't linger much longer. We can call an ambulance to take her to the hospital or check with the doctor about comfort measures we can take here. Does she have a DNR order?"

Annie's heart was beating so fast she could hardly take in the question. "You mean a Do Not Resuscitate?"

Carolee nodded.

"Yes." Annie's thoughts were going in a million directions. It was too soon. This couldn't be happening. But it was. She struggled to hold on to her emotions. "She…" Her throat constricted. "She…wanted to be here. For the end."

"Then that's the way it will be. Let's phone the doctor. Then I'll call home and let them know I'm staying with you."

Annie was stunned. "You'd do that?"

"Of course. What are friends for?"

Then the tears came, gushing from aching places Annie hadn't known existed.

CHAPTER NINE

THE SUN SHIMMERED. Puffy whiter-than-white clouds floated lazily across an azure sky. Like an invitation, the songs of seabirds sounded more plaintive than raucous. Geneva smiled, relaxing into the scene. If only she could reach out her hand, she could surely touch the cottony substance of the clouds or skim over the tops of the blue-green waves rolling, rolling toward the shore. The sound came again. Hoarse and insistent. From somewhere inside her?

She struggled to open her eyes. But her lids were so very heavy. The foam-tipped breakers meeting the shore played lulling music, almost impossible to resist.

"Auntie G.!"

Warmth. A caress. She flailed, summoning consciousness. Someone. Someone important. A spasm shook her. When she opened her eyes, the seascape vanished. For a moment she considered closing them again, giving in to the siren lure of the majestic ocean. But the call came again.

"Auntie G.! It's Annie."

A hand clasped hers. Fingers lightly brushed her forehead. In a voice she didn't recognize as hers, she whispered, "Petunia?"

The dear, dear face of her great-niece nearly filled her range of vision, those hazel eyes overflowing with love. Behind Annie, she barely made out other faces. One lined and familiar. Carmen. Tears leaked from Geneva's eyes.

In the distance, the cry of gulls. The lap of water on sand.

"Señorita."

Geneva turned her head. The companion of her days. Why did these women look so sad? Couldn't they see the clouds or hear the wash of waves swirling through tide pools?

"Auntie G., you've been my anchor. I love you so."

"Love." With great effort she found the next word. "Too."

She tasted salt air on her lips. Then, borne on the sea breeze, another voice summoned her, lilting, joyous. "Geneva! Sis! I'm waiting."

Across the beach he came, running toward her, his arms flung wide in welcome, his hair tousled, a cherubic smile lighting his features. She knew him. She started running, slowly at first, then faster and faster. "Caleb!" She couldn't contain herself, laughing with delight as the space between them narrowed.

For the flicker of an instant, she thought she heard someone say, "She's gone." Then, in a miracle, her brother's arms enclosed her and the two of them floated weightless high above the sea.

AFTERWARD, Annie had no recollection of how long she sat by Geneva's bedside. Not even when Carolee finally led her into the kitchen, wrapped her in a blanket and set a cup of piping-hot tea in front of her. Through the night her tears had dried to dust, making it nearly impossible to speak.

Carmen was doing what she always did—taking care of others. She rolled biscuit dough on the breadboard, occasionally dabbing at her eyes with her apron. Under her breath, she intoned the Lord's Prayer in Spanish. After encouraging Annie to drink the tea, with a nod toward Carmen, Carolee picked up the phone and disappeared into the living room. As if from a very great distance, Annie could make out snippets of Carolee's conversation. The doctor. The mortuary. "No, I'm sorry. I can't make it in for my shift today," she heard Carolee explain, she supposed to her nursing supervisor.

Tea. She took another mouthful. The drink she had always shared with Auntie G. Even though Carmen worked quietly just a few feet from her and Carolee was taking care of the necessary details, Annie felt totally alone. She shivered, drawing the blanket closer around her shoulders. She had lived in dread of this moment, but never had she imagined the depth of her grief. Of course, she had mourned before, but this time, she had been present when death came with overwhelming immediacy.

And yet…with such beauty. Such dignity. Through these few weeks, Auntie G. had put up a valiant fight, saving her energy to expend on Annie's behalf. A last gift. The end itself had been…spiritual. That was the only word for it. In that final moment of recognition and farewell, Geneva had expressed love, her face infused with color, all stress fading, a beatific smile gracing her lips. As bereft as Annie felt, she could not begrudge her aunt such a swift, serene passage.

Carolee came into the kitchen, pulling a stool next to Annie's. "I've phoned the doctor and the funeral home." She went over the thrust of those conversations. "Is there anyone else you'd like me to call?"

Annie's body shook with the force of her sigh. "Not right now." Later she would notify the attorney, Nina Valdez, and Geneva's publisher. She picked up the mug, slipped from her seat and walked to Auntie G.'s favorite bay window. Dawn was streaking the eastern sky. Looking to the west, she watched the ocean become more and more distinct as morning sunlight slowly dappled the water. Auntie G. had loved this view with its constantly changing elements—light and shadow, calm and storm. The Pacific. For the first time this morning, Annie smiled. Pacific. Peaceful.

She took another sip of tea, relishing the warmth. A new day. One full of arrangements and legalities. But in this moment, all was quiet. Carolee had asked if there was anyone Annie wanted her to call.

There was one. But that was a call she had to make herself. And only when she could control her own need to have Kyle's arms around her.

GENEVA HAD NOT WANTED an organized religious service. "I've traveled the world, Annie," she had explained, "and so far as I've seen, no one religion has a corner on the spiritual path. I've been in cathedrals, synagogues, mosques, ashrams and temples. The Creator is everywhere. Please don't invite a horde of people. A simple sunset gathering of friends on the beach will be the perfect send-off."

And so, two days after Geneva died, on a beautiful May evening, a small group gathered—Carmen, Nina, Kyle, Carolee and her husband, Frances and her daughter, Dr. Woodruff, Geneva's attorney, her New York editor, a few elderly townspeople and Annie. A friend of Carolee's husband brought his guitar and played softly as people gathered at the water's edge. Draped around her shoulders, Annie wore a colorful Indian shawl Geneva had favored. In her hands, she cradled a tall, delicate vase Auntie G. had purchased in Tokyo—one she had selected to hold her great-aunt's ashes.

When the last haunting notes of the guitar faded, Annie welcomed everyone and invited those who wished to offer a special memory of Geneva Greer to speak. She was touched by the doctor's remarks concerning her respect for Geneva's courage in the face of death, by Frances's tribute to the enduring quality of Geneva's friendship, by the uplifting comments of her editor, and, most especially, by Carmen's words. "*Señorita,* she love me like a sister. How would I, a poor woman, have ever seen so much of this world without her? For me, it was privilege to serve such a one. Unselfish. Steady. And so I say to my beloved sister, *vaya con Dios.*"

After a long silence, Annie, too choked up to utter a word, simply nodded to Carmen, who began, "Our Father…" The blended voices, as others joined in, lifted Annie as if on wings. After the "Amen," she slipped off her shoes and walked barefoot to the water's edge. The others followed, forming a semicircle around her. "My aunt Geneva was a traveler. More than anything she loved the smells, the sounds, the sights of exotic places. She never met a stranger and shared her joy of living with all whom she met. Now she is on her last, great adventure—a voyage to the most beautiful place of all. She asked that we scatter her ashes in the vast and boundless ocean that she loved so passionately. And so now we commit our precious Geneva to the sea."

With a heavy sigh, Annie waded knee-deep into the water, which swirled around her legs, the sandy ocean bottom shifting slightly beneath her. Hesitating, she took in the scene—the dear ones gathered around her, the splendor of the sunset, the sparkle of the waters that would embrace the ashes and carry them to distant lands. Then she plunged her hand into the soft powder, the essence of a life, and cast the particles into the air, finally upending the vase to send the last of Auntie G. to the four corners of the globe. She stood quietly, anticipating the end of the service. But instead of raised voices, the one she heard was much deeper and achingly familiar. Kyle's rich baritone.

"Sunset and evening star,
And one clear call for me!
And may there be no moaning of the bar,
When I put out to sea."

Incredulous, she slowly turned, listening to the words of Tennyson's immortal "Crossing the Bar."

He glanced up from the book he held in his hands,

and their eyes met. In that moment it was as if Auntie G. stood beside her smiling and saying, "See, I told you he's a good man."

The words of the poem washed over her.

"Twilight and evening bell,
And after that the dark!
And may there be no sadness of farewell,
When I embark.
For though from out our bourne of Time and Place
The flood may bear me far,
I hope to see my Pilot face to face
When I have crossed the bar."

When Kyle finished, he closed the book and walked toward Annie, stopping beside her and gently relieving her of the vase.

At that moment the guitarist spontaneously began singing. "Amazing grace, how sweet the sound…" As others joined in, the golden orb of the sun slipped beneath the horizon. "Safe travels, Auntie G.," Annie whispered.

The mourners then turned and walked silently toward the cottage where a supper, lovingly prepared by Carmen, awaited. Near the porch, Annie hung back, letting the others go ahead. She reached out and stopped Kyle, her hand on his chest. "How did you know? Who…?"

"Your aunt and I had several private conversations before she died. Last week she sent me a letter. She must've sensed the end was near. In it, she enclosed the poem and told me how much it would mean to her if I read it today. When Carolee told me Geneva had passed away, she also said you weren't accepting calls. But, Annie, I want you to know something." His gray eyes, now tinged with a blue so like the sea, fixed on hers. "I would have been at the service. For you."

Her hand lingered on his chest, as if the connection grounded her. For the first time in these past few days, she knew peace.

"She left the cottage to me," Annie said softly.

He nodded. "That must be why she was so anxious to have the repairs made. Will you keep it?"

Her hand dropped to her side and she turned to look at the house, the soft lights in the windows welcoming. "I don't know."

The spell was broken when Kyle stepped back, his eyes never leaving hers. "I, uh, I'll be going now. You have my card, my numbers. If you need anything, anything at all—"

She finished for him. "I'll call."

BUT SHE DIDN'T. Kyle rationalized that Annie had Carmen and others to help her or that when they'd bid Auntie G. farewell, his work with the Greers was finished. But in his heart he knew better. Without an excuse to show up at the cottage, he was forced to turn the spotlight on his true motives. He needed to see that she was all right. But it was more than that. Much more.

He went through the motions at work, then lost sleep at night debating what to do. He'd sit in his darkened living room, holding Pete's letter in his hand, as if its mute testimony was an indictment. Why couldn't he give it to her? Get it over with? The answer came from his gut. Would whatever Pete wrote turn Annie's thoughts to the past? Ruin any connection between Annie and him? Bottom line, he was in love with her and terrified of breaking the fragile bond they'd forged.

Like flames licking at kindling, guilt curled around him, a hot blaze. Had Pete known about the stolen embrace? About Kyle's mute adoration of his friend's girl? Could he have been more encouraging and helpful in those years when Pete tried so hard to locate Annie? And, for God's sake, why hadn't he been more alert, instead of sitting there in that Humvee looking at the mountains when that Afghani sniper was sighting Pete in his crosshairs?

Mornings were no better. He'd tuck the letter back in his drawer, then, red-eyed from lack of sleep, he'd head for work, preoccupied. Miserable.

Saturday came, yawning before him, empty of purpose. Not that he hadn't had offers. Wade Hanson had invited him to go fishing. Bruce had suggested a round of golf. Bubba seemed to be avoiding him and his foul mood, slinking under the kitchen table or dozing on the sofa.

Stepping out of the shower that morning, he knew he couldn't continue living in this purgatory. What could it hurt to check on Annie? A neighborly gesture. He pulled on a clean pair of jeans and a navy-blue long-sleeved knit shirt. The morning was cool, so he grabbed a windbreaker and whistled for Bubba. "C'mon, sport. We're going for a ride."

Bubba leaped from his perch on the sofa and padded eagerly toward the door.

"Yeah, I know I've been a surly bastard. It's time to do something about that. Cross your paws, buddy. Nothing's certain where women are concerned."

ANNIE HAD BEEN UP since dawn, determined to box up Auntie G.'s clothes and personal belongings. Carmen had delayed her departure until the day after the memorial service, and Carolee had been faithfully checking in on Annie after work. But, oddly, the solitude she had feared was a blessing. Surrounded by the furnishings and treasures she had loved ever since she was tiny, she felt Auntie G.'s comforting presence. Annie had given herself time before determining the course of her future. The house was hers. She could stay. The attorney, however, had told her it was Geneva's wish that it be sold if that was what Annie wanted. He said she'd called it "Annie's seed money."

She was torn. The cottage was home. Eden Bay was not, yet gradually she was finding it more difficult to imagine herself anyplace else. As she opened the bottom drawer of Auntie G.'s bureau and began sorting the nightgowns and robes, she promised herself she'd think about the future another day. Carefully she laid the garments on the bed, inhaling the unique fragrance that was Auntie G., longing for one more game of gin rummy, one more family story, one more hug.

She'd finished with the bureau and was starting on the closet, unaware of the tearstains on her cheeks, when she heard a knock on the door. She ran her hands through her hair, wiped her nose and made her way to the front hall, wondering who would be stopping by. When she opened the door, she was startled to see Kyle.

"You never called," he said gently.

Her heartbeat accelerated to double time. "No, I didn't."

Neither moved for the longest time. "May I come in?"

As if recovering from a trance, she remembered her manners. "Oh, I'm sorry, it's just that…I'm not thinking quite straight lately."

"Understandable," he said, crossing the threshold.

She'd forgotten how big he was. How his broad shoulders blocked the sun and how his solid chest was the perfect place to lay a weary head.

He brushed a hand over her hair. "How are you?" he asked in a way that convinced her he wanted the truth.

"It's rough. Very rough."

It was then that he reached out. Then that she caved into the overwhelming need she had of him. She wrapped her arms around his neck so tightly she feared she would strangle him, lost in the sensation of his broad hands caressing her back, his sturdy legs bracing them both against the onslaught of her emotion. To be warm, safe, comforted, cherished—stars burst behind her closed lids and she felt every muscle in her body relax as Kyle held her, murmuring her name over and over.

Then, in a synchronous movement, their lips met in a breathless kiss, which deepened and increased in intensity. Annie's knees buckled, but Kyle supported her, his mouth urgently exploring hers. Time fell away. She was lost in the smell, the feel and the taste of this man. Until…

When his fingers grazed her breast, like the click of

an automatic switch, she turned to ice, pushing him away, hearing her voice cry raggedly, "No!"

His muffled words barely penetrated the dizziness filling her head. "Annie? I'm sorry. What is it?"

She turned away, leaning over with her hands on her knees, inhaling deep breaths. "Please, just don't touch me. Not…like that."

"My God, Annie, I didn't mean to hurt you. I would never do that. Here, let me help you to a chair."

Like a dazed victim, she permitted him to lead her to the living room sofa.

"Can I get you anything?"

She shook her head, flushed with shame and overcome by revulsion. She buried her head in her hands, powerless to avoid the image crowding her brain. She felt the man sit down next to her, but he did not touch her. Only waited.

She clamped her arms around her stomach, rocking back and forth, willing calm. Outside the window, a gentle rain had begun. *Cleansing.* She felt hysterical laughter building in her chest. That's what Auntie G. had called it. *God's cleansing.* A harsh sound ripped from her lips. She would never be clean.

"Annie? Something is very wrong. Has someone hurt you?"

She made the mistake in that moment of looking at Kyle, his face drawn with worry, his eyes searching for answers. And instead of purging herself of bile, a torrent of words came, one piling on top of the other, forced from somewhere in the most hidden part of her. She tried, but was helpless to stop them as they spewed forth in a thundering cataract.

"He raped me!"

"Who did?"

"George. My stepfather. He...he wouldn't leave me alone. He kept creeping into the bedroom at night. Smiling and rubbing my arm and telling me I was his kitten. He'd buy me these awful slinky nightgowns, but I'd hide them. 'Try one on for Georgie,' he'd say. He hadn't really done anything then, so I thought I could get away when I went off to summer school, but—" a giant wrenching gasp escaped her "—it was too late."

"Son of a bitch," she heard Kyle mutter, but he didn't take his eyes off her. "Go on. Let it out, Annie."

As if she could help herself. "After the graduation party, I came home. Everything was quiet. Pete had kissed me good-night and left me at the door. I was so happy, yet sad, too, because he was leaving for Guard camp. I brushed my teeth, put on my pajamas and went to bed, all the while thinking of my Pete. I must've dozed, because suddenly I felt a hand rubbing my breasts and then fumbling with my pajama bottoms. I could smell him before I saw him. The bourbon breath, the cigar smoke clinging to his robe. When I opened my eyes, he grinned, all the while slipping his hand inside my pants, fumbling my crotch. I started to scream, but he clamped a hand over my mouth. 'There, there, my beautiful one. Just lie still. Be good to Georgie. This won't hurt a bit.'"

Kyle wrapped his arm around her and hugged her to his chest. But still she couldn't stop. "Then he untied the belt of his robe and in the moonlight I could see his hairy chest, and then that...that thing. Big. I tried to get away, I really did." In her mind's eye she pictured the struggle. But he was too strong. With one hand he spread her legs and with the other he aroused himself. Her screams brought no one. "He was out of his mind, nothing was going to stop him, not my begging, my prayers or my screams." She paused, took a deep breath, and then her tone turned cold. "When he finished, he fell on top of me. 'There's more where that came from, princess,' he said."

"Annie, honey, my God, I'm so sorry. If he wasn't already dead, I'd kill the son of a bitch." Kyle's face was pale, grim, his jaw working.

Like an eruption, the tears came then, convulsing Annie. Kyle's words were echoes of Pete's promise. But no one could have stopped George. In a moment of awful revelation, Annie acknowledged that she was damaged goods, not just because she'd been raped, but because she now recoiled from any man's touch, even Kyle's. A heavy, heavy price. Through her sobs, she managed to say brokenly, "Oh, no, Kyle, I'm the one who's sorry."

"You have nothing to apologize for. It wasn't your fault, Annie. You have to believe that."

But could she? Had she subconsciously done something to lead George on? Was she partly to blame? Maybe she should have bought a lock for her bedroom door. Run away sooner. Called Auntie G. no matter how many miles separated them. Yet at the time, she remembered thinking she was totally dependent upon her stepfather. She couldn't afford to alienate him. He was paying for college—her only means of escape.

"You didn't tell Pete he raped you?"

She straightened up. Kyle handed her his handkerchief and she blew her nose. "I couldn't. He knew I was having trouble with George. He…he said he'd kill him if he touched me."

"And he would have."

"I know. That's why I couldn't say anything. That's why I ran away from Eden Bay so suddenly the morning before you and Pete left for Guard camp. Besides, I was damaged goods. Who would've wanted me after what happened?"

"Christ." Kyle raked a hand across his head in frustration, then bundled Annie even closer. "It's over, Annie. A long time ago. Let me help you heal."

"You'd do that?" She could hardly trust herself to look at him. The love in his eyes was blinding.

"In a heartbeat."

They sat entwined for a very long time, Kyle soothing her with gentle kisses and caresses, the kind a loving parent would bestow on an injured child. Finally she sat up and glanced around as if getting her bearings. "Please. Don't leave."

His fingers grazed her cheek tenderly. "I won't. Not until you ask me to."

That was the day they spent hours walking on the beach, uttering only an occasional word. Because everything had been said. All they needed now was the shared silence of friendship.

Before Kyle left late that afternoon at Annie's request, he stood close to her, holding both of her hands. After staring intently into her eyes, he said, "Please, Annie, stay in Eden Bay."

IT WAS ONLY when Kyle got into the truck that he gave full vent to his pent-up fury. Bubba shrank against the passenger door as curse after curse reverberated through the cab. Kyle had never felt so damn helpless in his entire life. The hell of it was he didn't even have a target for his rage—that son of a bitch George had died before anyone could punish him. Hell, folks in Eden Bay still regarded the former bank president with respect. The irony of it made him pound the steering wheel in frustration. For anyone, anyone, to lay a finger on Annie was unthinkable. It was a heinous crime done under the shadow of darkness by a cowardly monster. Shit! Shit! Shit!

He had calmed down only slightly by the time he pulled into his own driveway. No wonder Annie had fled Eden Bay. If only she had told Pete. The two of them would have hauled George's ass straight to the police station, if they hadn't killed him first. Kyle sat staring into the distance, idly scratching Bubba between the ears. "Sorry for the outburst, fella. But that creep hurt our Annie badly." Bubba growled in response. "I know, boy. You'd have sunk your teeth into the jerk."

As he and Annie had strolled the beach this afternoon, he'd been nearly overcome by the sacrifices she had made to save Pete from doing something rash and to help him realize his dream of serving in the Guard. He shook his head in disbelief. She must've loved him very much.

She had, for all intents and purposes, buried herself in Arizona, terrified of George and convinced the scandal of her disappearance was unforgivable. What courage it must have taken for her to return to Eden Bay to care for her great-aunt. And what love.

All Kyle wanted to do was protect and heal her, love her back to her outgoing, sunny self. But he was unsure how to do that. She was as skittish as a fawn, and as much as he craved a physical relationship with her, she was nowhere near ready. Just as with a frightened animal, he first had to win her trust—and hope that somewhere down the line she would welcome his touch and respond to his intense need of her.

Finally, he got out of his truck and headed for the house where, he remembered guiltily, Pete's letter waited to be delivered.

A letter that could change so much.

When he entered his house, the flashing red light on the answering machine drew his attention. He debated about listening to the message. But it could be Annie.

Reluctantly he pressed Play. Margaret's voice filled the room. There was no question about her frame of mind. "It wasn't enough for you to break my sister's heart. No other woman? Explain then why Rosemary saw you walking on the beach today with Annie Greer. Holding hands, no less. Kyle, you could have chosen anyone else in the whole world. But Annie? Some friend of Pete's you are!"

At that point she had hung up.

He sank onto the sofa. He had no defense. Margaret was right. There was another woman, the last one the Nemecs would ever accept. And one he knew he could never give up.

Pete, buddy, what am I supposed to do?

CHAPTER TEN

AT THE END of the second week following Geneva's death, the boutique in Scottsdale called requesting additional handmade purses. Although the timing couldn't have been worse, Annie seized the opportunity. Work was the only thing that kept grief and looming decisions at bay. Nothing, however, had kept her time with Kyle from intruding into her thoughts. Since the day when she'd spewed out her awful story, he had called twice, but she had declined to see him. First she had to sort herself out and come to some decisions about what she really wanted.

On this unseasonably warm Sunday morning, she had opened the windows, letting fresh air blow through the house. Now, sitting at her worktable fingering a pale green satin, a lush midnight-blue velvet and a sturdy brocade, she closed her eyes, trying to picture how she could reproduce the colors of a seascape in fabric. As if they had minds of their own, her hands began shifting the pieces, rearranging, pulling other swatches from the pile until she could see exactly how to begin. In the act of creating, she lost track of time until she glanced at the clock. Two hours had passed since she'd given conscious thought to anything but the piece in front of her. That wasn't much, but it was her first indication that, in jerks and tugs, healing might eventually be possible.

Despite invitations from Carolee and Geneva's friend Frances, she'd spent last week by herself in the cottage, continuing to sort through Geneva's things and giving in to periodic bouts of grief. Annie had been alone for so many years that to come back to Eden Bay and feel such a family connection with Auntie G.... She couldn't indulge that train of thought. These last weeks here with Geneva were too immediate, and her emotions were all over the place.

Before Nina returned to Bisbee after the service, she had cautioned Annie. "You're in no condition right now to make major decisions. You have the house and your inheritance, so there is no urgency. Please take all the time you need. Meanwhile, I will keep your apartment in Bisbee until you decide what the future holds."

Thoughts of the future were never far away. Pounding in her brain with maddening insistence were Kyle's final words to her last weekend: "Stay in Eden Bay."

But how could she? The cottage was one thing, but Eden Bay was a different matter. Other than Carolee and Kyle, and a nodding acquaintance with Frances, she had no friends. The Nemecs had no use for her. Familiar scenes around town were painfully reminiscent either of wonderful, carefree times with Pete or the nightmare of George. Carolee could talk all she wanted about the past being the past, but memories were long and gossip lurked at every turn. It should be easy to make the first, most obvious decision—to leave Eden Bay. But it wasn't.

Outside the window gulls circled and cried. In the distance she could faintly hear the tolling of a church bell. In truth, though, the only familiar, safe world she knew was in this house. The cottage was the one place where she had always felt loved. How could she sell out, never to return to this haven?

And how could she say goodbye to Kyle? Her heart sank. She knew she was fighting the attraction she felt for him. It would be all too easy to give in, to let him coddle and protect her. But any man would want more than that. Much more. Given all that had happened to her, she didn't think she could give it, didn't think her body would cooperate even if her mind desired greater intimacy.

Then there was Pete. Was she using Kyle as a surrogate for him? A convenient fill-in, and because of their shared past, a particularly comfortable one?

She buried her head in her hands. Thanks to George, since Pete, she had not felt attracted to a man. After the rape she had considered herself dead in that regard. Cold, unresponsive, neutered. Then, out of the blue, had come Kyle's one kiss and the sparks that had electrified her, even as she simultaneously shrank from the gentle brush of his fingers on her breast. In that one touch, she had been immediately transported to her darkened bedroom where she had huddled, recoiling from George. Would the image of her stepfather always be there, intruding into her life? Rendering her incapable of giving love? She shoved back her chair and stood, raging at George. How dare he ruin her life? Control her future?

Moving to the window, she let the breeze cool her flushed face. She didn't know if she had the patience or the will to fight the past. But she wanted to. Oh, how she wanted to.

KYLE FIRED UP the lawn mower Sunday afternoon and attacked his small, neglected yard. As he made monotonous trips back and forth across the lawn, he arrived at a conclusion: the time had come for honesty—with Annie and with the Nemecs. In the office Rosemary spoke to him only when necessary. He was clearly persona non grata with the female branch of the family. How could he continue accepting Bruce's generosity, knowing he'd hurt Rosemary and, worse yet, without acknowledging his vigilance might have prevented Pete's death? For six years, he'd buried the truth—that he was as culpable as anyone. That he'd let his own need for family and security sway his judgment. Until the Nemecs, he had never had a frame of reference for either family or home.

During Kyle's childhood, his father had taken every opportunity to remind him that his "no-good hot pants of a mother" had run off with another man, abandoning them when Kyle was three. As a boy, Kyle would sit on the stoop waiting for the mailman, hoping that this time the letter would come—the one from his mother, saying that she'd made a mistake, missed her son and loved him very much. Of course, that letter never arrived.

To Rosemary and Margaret now, it must seem as if

he were as heartless as his mother, a thought that sickened him. Margaret's most recent phone message had corroborated that image of him. Sometimes he wondered if he was even capable of love.

Finished with the mowing, he set the machine aside and picked up the edger. Sweat dampened his shirt as he attacked the tall grass around the trees and abutting the mobile home. He'd tried to respect Annie's need for space, even though being rebuffed when he'd phoned was tough to take. Yet she couldn't hide forever in that cottage. He knew she was scared. If he wanted to move their relationship to the next level, he would have to be patient and take his signals from her.

But before any of that could happen, he would have to show her Pete's letter. It was not his place to keep it from her, not if he had any integrity at all. Pete had never shared the contents with him, so he had no idea what the consequences would be—whether or not Pete's words would deep-six any hopes Kyle had for a future with Annie. He was long accustomed to rejection, but this time the prospect terrified him.

He put the lawn tools in the storage shed and went into the house. Bubba followed as he stripped off his clothes and stepped into the shower. He stayed there a long time, letting the hot water pummel him. Finally he made a decision.

Stepping out of the shower, he pulled on his briefs, then spoke. "Bubba, we're men of action, right? It's time I paid a call on Miss Annie Greer. You with me?"

A thump of the dog's tail on the floor was all the encouragement Kyle needed.

WHEN KYLE TURNED into the driveway, he spotted Annie sitting on the porch swing, her legs drawn up and a large sweatshirt pulled over her knees. She looked up, her body tensing. Maybe he should've called. *Great idea, Becker. And risk rejection again?*

As he ambled up the walk and mounted the porch steps, she didn't move. "The phone calls weren't working for me," he said, lounging against the porch rail opposite her.

"I didn't intend to be so abrupt when you called," Annie said, touching her toe to the porch floor to set the swing in motion. "It was thoughtful of you to concern yourself."

"You aren't a 'concern,' Annie. I care about you."

"You've always been a good friend. First to Pete, now to me."

He wanted to cry out that he wanted more, but if friendship was the starting point, then so be it. "I'm wondering if you're spending too much time alone."

"That's kind of a habit of mine."

"It didn't used to be."

She stilled the swing. "No, I suppose not. But so much has changed."

"Bad things have happened, Annie, but inside of you is still the girl Pete fell in love with." *That I fell in love with.* "Don't go through this all by yourself. Let me be here for you."

She stretched out her arms and closed her eyes. Kyle knew she was buying time before answering. Then, in a complete non sequitur, she asked him if he played gin rummy. He nodded. He couldn't count the hours whiled

away at cards in Afghanistan. She rose to her feet.
"Great. Let's see if you're any good."

WHEN TWILIGHT CAME, they finally gave up gin rummy.
"Would you like to join me for supper?" Annie asked
as she scooped up the cards.

"Sure I wouldn't be intruding?"

She reached for his hand. "Please."

In the dim light, he studied her face, then seemed to
come to a conclusion. "If you're certain…"

The tentativeness of their conversation and the sub-
text of longing weren't lost on her. "I'm sure."

He stood. "Good. I'll let Bubba out of the truck for
a run." He placed a warm hand on her shoulder. "Don't
go anyplace. I'll be back soon."

Annie moved to the kitchen, mentally planning a
simple menu of grilled cheese sandwiches, pasta salad
and sliced tomatoes. As she set a pot of water to boil for
the bow tie pasta, she realized how few meals she'd
eaten in the past several days. It had been easier to snack
on cereal and fruit.

Kyle came in as she was readying the sandwiches for
the grill. "Can I help?"

She handed him a knife. "Thanks. You could slice
the tomatoes."

Neither of them said anything, working in companionable silence. He sliced tomatoes with the same ease
he drove a nail. When he moved behind her to rinse the
knife at the sink, she could smell the Irish Spring smell
of him, sense the heat radiating from his body. She experienced the same involuntary rush she had when he'd

first kissed her. If only she could welcome her body's natural reaction instead of anticipating the physical withdrawal she knew lay ahead.

Kyle was rummaging in one of the drawers. "Aha!" he said, pulling out three candles. "I spotted some candlesticks earlier. What do you say we dine alfresco, as they say on the cooking shows?"

"You watch cooking shows?"

"If there's no game I'm interested in, sure." He cocked his head. "So? Do you think it's too cool outside?"

"By all means, alfresco it is."

While he set the table on the porch, she drained the pasta, tossed it with tuna, mayonnaise and pickle relish and then began grilling the sandwiches.

He had arranged the candles in the center of the table and located a bottle of red wine in Auntie G.'s liquor cabinet. Before eating, she held up her goblet for him to fill. After he'd helped himself, she raised her glass in a toast. "To better tomorrows."

"To better tomorrows," he echoed.

Small talk carried them through dinner. Kyle asked her how she had gotten started in the purse-making business. She inquired about his remodeling projects. By the time she'd cleared the table and stacked the dishes in the sink, she was out of topics of conversation. She arranged apples, grapes and cheese on a board and carried them back out to the porch. "Dessert. I'll do better next time."

Kyle had moved his chair beside hers, so both faced the ocean. "I hope there will be a next time." He laid an arm on the back of her chair.

Night had fallen and, one by one, stars appeared in the dark sky. "I can't promise anything."

"I understand that. I'm a patient man."

To cover her nervousness, she picked up a small bunch of grapes and popped one in her mouth. "I don't know, Kyle. I'm really out of practice. Then there's…you know…the past."

"Unless you want to talk about it again, I'll never bring it up." He brushed back a tendril of hair that had fallen across her cheek. "You deserve so much more, Annie." Then he took the grapes from her, leaned forward and brushed his lips lightly but lingeringly over hers.

She held her breath, her body taut with expectation, but the kiss, so gentle and loving, felt just right. When he pulled away and she could breathe again, she whispered, "It's scary. All I can promise is that I will try."

"That's good enough for me."

He picked up her hand and held it while they listened to the ebb and flow of the waves, shushing and hissing.

When he stood to leave, he drew her close. "Will you let me hold you?"

She stepped into his arms, laid her head against his chest and permitted his strength and warmth to envelop her. It was a good place to be, she decided. A very good place. If only she could step out of the shadow of the past.

His lips grazed her cheek before he released her. "Good night, sweet Annie."

"Good night," she whispered.

She stood on the porch, watching until the taillights of his truck were mere pinpoints. Her body vibrated with need of him. She hugged herself against the promise of her arousal and the reality of her fear. *Oh, Auntie G. Help me. I don't want to be half a woman for this man.*

KYLE WAS nearly home when he came to his senses. The time with Annie had been so perfect, so peaceful, he hadn't wanted to spoil the mood by giving her the letter tucked in his back pocket. He'd been totally pumped when she'd promised to give their relationship a chance. And now the damn letter. How far could he let things go without giving it to her? He knew the answer. Not far.

He pulled to the side of the road and made a U-turn. It was never going to get any easier, so he might as well do it now. He owed it to Pete and to Annie. Regardless of his own feelings, he had to put them first.

Lights were still on in the cottage when he pulled into the driveway. After he drew to a stop and stepped out of the cab, he stood by the truck, one hand on the door, debating still. He could change his mind. Annie would never have to know. Pete was gone. How could anything he might have written make a difference now? With a shake of his head, he recognized the source of his hesitation. He didn't want anything, not even Pete, to come between him and Annie.

Just then the porch light flicked on and Annie stood framed in the doorway. "Kyle?" Her voice floated on the night air.

"Yeah, it's me." He lumbered up the porch steps. "I didn't mean to startle you."

"I thought you might have forgotten something. I did."

"You did?"

Barefoot, she stepped onto the porch and walked

straight into his arms. Her mouth found his, tasting, probing, and when their tongues met, he braced himself against the porch rail, reveling in the feel of her small, soft breasts pressed tight against his chest. He lifted her off her feet, the better to hold her. When she drew back, framing his face in her hands, her eyes were glowing. "I thought I needed to demonstrate that I'm willing to try." Then she let her body slide along his until her feet found the floor. All the time, he was caressing her back, her hair. "Did I do okay?" she asked as if there could be any doubt.

"You did just fine. Much more of that and you'll drive me crazy."

Her lilting giggle, a sound he hadn't heard in years, filled him with joy. Could he be the man to heal the wounds inflicted by that bastard? He sure wanted a chance to find out.

She laid a hand on his arm. "Did *you* forget something?"

Like a pin pricking a balloon, elation drained out of him. The moment of truth had come, and there was nothing he could do to make it go away.

"Yes, I did."

The light went out of her eyes and worry lines creased her forehead. "This doesn't sound good. I don't know how much more bad news I can take."

"It's not bad, but it may be disturbing."

As if to delay the inevitable, she opened the porch door. "Let's go inside, then."

In the living room, she perched on the edge of the sofa, poised to escape. "What is it, Kyle?"

Slowly he withdrew the envelope from his pocket and stood staring at the words *For Annie,* wishing that Pete had never died, that he'd never written the letter, that Kyle didn't care so deeply about the results and, above all, that Annie wouldn't have to endure any further hurt.

He held it out to her. "It's a letter from Pete."

Her gasp of surprise when she took it from him made his hands tremble. He thrust them into his pockets.

She stared at the words on the envelope. "I don't understand…. When? How?" She moved her fingers over the paper, tracing the letters of her name.

Kyle cleared his throat. "He gave it to me when we arrived in Afghanistan. You know…in case…" He could hardly go on. "In case something happened to him."

Her eyes rounded with misery then, in an abrupt change, darkened with anger. "Why are you just now giving it to me?" Her voice rose. "Once I came back to Eden Bay, how could you have just hung on to it like this?"

His face reddened with the effort to explain. "At first I was furious with you. You had disappeared and left Pete pining after you. When you showed up here, I thought it was the ultimate insult to his memory and to the Nemecs. I didn't figure you deserved whatever Pete had to say."

She stood, her face ashen. "That wasn't your decision to make."

He hung his head. "I know. I realize that." Finally, he dared to look into her eyes. "I love you, Annie. I don't want to lose you. But I guess it's all up to you now. And Pete."

She had drawn the envelope to her heart. Tears, in silent rebuke, rolled down her cheeks. "Pete was your friend," she said in a voice that tore him apart.

"Yes. I was wrong to withhold his letter. I'm sorry, Annie. Sorrier than you'll ever know."

"I think you should leave now."

"I'll let myself out."

"Do that."

He was halfway to the door when she uttered his name. He turned back to her. She remained rooted to the spot, clutching the letter. In a tinny voice she said, "I thought I could trust you."

His heart sank. "You can. Please, Annie, don't turn your back on me. Give me a chance to prove myself."

As if in slow motion, she shook her head. "I don't think I can."

There was nothing more he could say. He was left with an aching hollowness.

He drove slowly home. He'd never known such pain. Such powerlessness. He'd lost her.

As LIMP AS A RAG DOLL, Annie sank to the floor, her ears roaring with the thunder of her heartbeat. She could hardly breathe, so intense was the shock of holding in her hands a message from beyond the grave. *Pete.* The name boiled up from somewhere in her chest, a howl that broke the nighttime stillness.

Minutes passed, but Annie didn't move. Part of her wanted to rip into the envelope and lose herself in the familiar handwriting. She yearned to hear in his words the voice forever stilled. So long as she held the unopened envelope, though, the promise remained, the illusion that he was there in the room with her.

She foresaw, too, that whatever message the envelope contained, it would unleash a cataclysm of grief. She didn't know if she could bear it.

She had no time or sympathy for thoughts of Kyle and his attempt to play God. It was as if these past few weeks in Eden Bay had vanished into a time warp and she was back in high school—dancing in Pete's arms at the prom, running hand in hand through the surf with him, the two of them kissing breathlessly at her front door after a date. She closed her eyes and pictured Pete's face even as she realized she was seeing an eighteen-year-old, not the grown man he would have been now.

She rose from the floor, knowing there was only one place to read Pete's letter. With a cup of hot tea in Geneva's chair by the bay window. Auntie G.'s sanctuary. She prayed it would be hers, as well.

CHAPTER ELEVEN

ANNIE TURNED ON the reading lamp by Auntie G.'s chair and stared once more at the envelope. "For Annie." Dry mouthed, she carefully slit the flap and pulled out a single sheet of notebook paper. The abundance of words, all in Pete's handwriting, was nearly too much to take in. She took a minute to compose herself. Then she began reading.

My darling Annie,
I hope you never receive this letter because that would mean I'm not coming home to you. I can barely stand the thought that I will never see you again, that we will never be together as we'd always planned.

These past few years since you left have been hell. I've done everything I can do to find you. People tell me I should be angry, forget about you and move on with my life. I can't. That's all, I just can't. I don't have a clue how I know, but I just do—you're out there somewhere and you've never stopped loving me.

Annie lowered the letter to her lap. Her whole being swelled with gratitude that somehow her love for Pete had made its mysterious way to him. It defied reason, but she did believe that there was a communication that transcended time and space.

I remember so vividly holding you in my arms, how your body felt against mine. I've missed you terribly. You've always been the only girl for me.

We had such plans. How we'd marry and have children. How we'd introduce them to the miracle of tide pools, coastal forests and mountains. How we'd never let one day pass without telling them how much we loved them.

A flash of memory came. Of a time they'd lain on their stomachs, arms around each other, at the very edge of a tide pool, awed by the varieties of marine life visible in the swirling water. She could picture him looking over at her with a huge smile. "Way cool, huh?" he'd said. She remembered now how much she had loved the way even the simplest things delighted him. Mollusks, stars, volcanic rocks, anything. As if the universe had been prepared solely for his discovery and pleasure.

Well, sweetheart, if you're reading this, you know that our dreams are never going to come true. We had something very special between us and I'm so, so sorry to disappoint you like this.

There has never been a day since we met that I haven't loved you more than life itself. Even from where I am now, I hope you feel my love.

Annie shivered, as if a ghost had walked across her back. That tie of memory and devotion bound them both. No matter what else she might do in her life, she would never, ever forget Pete.

But I'm gone. That's not what we'd planned, but that's the way it is. Now, I want you to pay very close attention to what I'm about to say. Annie, oh, darling Annie, we had such beautiful dreams, but just because I can't live them, doesn't mean you shouldn't. More than anything, that's what I want for you—dreams. A good man to love and who will love you. Someone who will make you laugh, who will hold you close each night, who will give you children and grow old with you. I envy him at the same time that I pray for him to come to you. Live, Annie, live!

He'd signed the letter, "Always, your Pete." Tears blurred her vision, and for a few moments she nearly overlooked the P.S. on the back of the page.

Hey, if you don't have anyone particular in mind, I'll make a suggestion. Try my buddy Kyle. He needs a good woman, and you won't find anyone better to love.

That was so like Pete—to give his blessing from beyond the grave. But she couldn't think about Kyle right now. Tonight was for Pete. For honoring the person he'd been and the sacrifice he'd made. For mourning the love of her life and bidding farewell to old dreams.

Annie sat still for a long time. She was lost in memories, in the fading image of the fine young man she'd once loved.

Dawn was streaking the eastern sky before she finally folded the letter, replaced it in the envelope and made her way upstairs, where she fell, exhausted, across her bed.

KYLE HAD A MISERABLE WEEK. Nightmares that jolted him from a sound sleep into the chaos of memory and guilt. Days marked with jobs that didn't interest him. Hours of discomfort whenever he was around the Nemecs. How shabbily he'd repaid their friendship. First with Pete. Now with Annie.

Annie. Even thinking her name made him groan. No matter how many times he replayed last Sunday, the scenario always ended with her indictment of him: "I thought I could trust you." Clearly she hadn't changed her mind, because he hadn't heard from her all week. Not that he thought he would. Still…

Looking in the mirror Friday morning while he shaved, he could barely stand the sight of his own face. He'd been wrong. Flat-out wrong. And cowardly. He should have given Pete's letter to Annie the minute he knew she was back in Eden Bay. But no. He'd let first his anger at her and then his attraction to her govern his actions.

He studied his eyes reflected in the mirror. Bottom line, he was doing an ass-poor job of living with himself. He didn't know what he could do about Annie, but he sure as hell could do something about the Nemecs. By not telling them about his role in Pete's life—and death—he was living a lie. No matter the consequences, he needed to come clean with the family he'd come to love as his own.

As for Annie, the ball was in her court and there wasn't a thing he could do about that. But talking to the Nemecs was a start. He scrubbed a hand over his clean-shaven beard. He knew he was risking his job and their friendship again, but meeting with them was the only honorable course of action. Long overdue.

First thing after he arrived at work, he went to Bruce's office. When Kyle suggested the family meeting, Bruce raised an eyebrow. "This is important to you."

"Yes, sir. Very." He waited while Bruce phoned Janet, who insisted that Kyle join them all for Sunday dinner. Kyle swallowed, wondering how he'd be able to eat a morsel. "Thank you, Bruce."

Back in his cubicle, he buried his head in his hands. What he had to confess would upset the very people to whom he owed nearly everything. Was he being selfish? He could rethink this until he was blue in the face. Yet the fact remained: He wanted to be able to look at himself in the mirror.

BY SATURDAY MORNING, Annie couldn't count the number of times she'd reread Pete's words, memorizing phrases and letting his love reach out to her. The letter was a gift beyond price. This reopened grief, on top of that for Auntie G., should have been paralyzing. Yet for some strange reason it wasn't. It was as if the letter had put a voice to the past, to what she was mourning. In the sunny days and fresh breezes of the week, she'd been blessed by a kind of benediction—as if Pete had conspired with nature to write amen to this chapter of her life.

She'd even been able to work—finding solace and peace in the colors and textures of the fabrics, in the creative ideas that leaped unbidden to her mind. She loved sitting in this upstairs bedroom, the vast ocean just outside her window, making something new out of discarded materials. The permanence of the cottage, the miracle of the ever-changing seascape and the comfort of the familiar furnishings collected through the years by other Greers caused her to give increasingly serious thought to staying in Eden Bay. Maybe, like the poet Emily Dickinson, she could be an artist/recluse, a subject of eccentricity for the townsfolk.

But then there was Kyle.

For the umpteenth time, she shoved him from her mind, intent on finding just the right decorative stitch to use in joining a seam.

It was after eleven when she heard a thump on the front door and a voice calling out. "Annie Greer, are you in there?"

Grinning, Annie looked up from her work. Carolee. She leaned out the window. "I'm up here. I'll be down in a sec." She quickly tucked her denim shirt into her jeans and ran a brush through her hair.

Carolee, too, was dressed casually in leggings and an oversize shirt. She gave Annie a hug, then held her at arm's length. "Considering all you've been through, you look pretty darn good. Maybe a bit pale. It's time you got some fresh air."

"Pale, huh? I suppose I could get some sun."

"Great. Grab your purse and come on, then."

"Where are we going?"

"It's a surprise."

Annie usually didn't like surprises, but she followed Carolee to her car. In truth, it had been a week since she'd spoken with anyone except the checkout girl at the grocery store and Nina, who'd phoned to check on her. Carolee's radio was set on a station playing songs from the eighties, and they sang along as they drove south on the Coast Highway.

"Do I dare ask where you're taking me?"

"To lunch" was the only hint Carolee provided.

After fifteen minutes, Carolee wheeled off the highway into the parking lot of a seaside restaurant with a large deck suspended at the edge of a cliff overlooking the Pacific. "We're here," she announced. "I'm starving for some fried halibut."

As if on cue, Annie's stomach growled. "I guess I am, too. Lead on."

They walked through the dining room and out onto the deck with its breathtaking view. Colorful beach umbrellas shaded each table. When Annie looked in the direction the hostess was heading, she froze to the spot, all pleasure draining from her. Seated at the large table were four other women—wearing the grown-up faces

of girls she'd known at Eden Bay High. She thought she
might hyperventilate. She couldn't do this—join them
and deal with their questions.

Sensing her distress, Carolee slid an arm around her.
"It's okay, Annie," she whispered. "Really. These are
your friends. I would never put you in an uncomfortable
situation."

All four women stood as they approached, smiles
wreathing their faces. One by one, she recognized them.
Mary Hocker, a fellow cheerleader; Lindsey O'Neal, her
chem lab partner; Jill Sutherland, her locker mate; and
Betsy Dale, her next-door neighbor in the house on Kittiwake. Before she could say anything, she was engulfed
by hugs and excited hellos.

When Annie finally caught her breath and sat down,
she realized that not one single person had an accusa-
tory look in her eye. In fact, they heaped warm greet-
ings on her. "Sorry about your aunt." "We're so glad
you're back in Eden Bay." "We've missed you, Annie." "Not fair. How come you look just like you did
in high school, and I have stretch marks and thirty
extra pounds?"

She heard all about their husbands, jobs and children.
Not one of them said, "Where have you been all these
years?" or "How could you break Pete's heart like that?"

By dessert, she found herself relaxing, then talking
about her purse business. Mary asked if she could come
by the house and see some samples. She was in charge
of an upcoming charity event and thought offering some
purses for auction would give Annie wide local exposure.

As if Annie had something to contribute. No matter

how genuinely interested they seemed in her or how desperately she wanted to be included in their circle, the fact remained: there was an elephant in the room.

An elephant called running away.

Carolee insisted on paying her tab. "After all, I spirited you here under false pretenses."

"But good ones, I hope," Lindsey said, studying Annie's face with concern.

Not now. The tears couldn't come now. She collected herself. "Yes, good ones."

She was quiet for the first miles of the ride home. Reflecting, she realized how much it meant to be embraced by these friends from the past. She had steeled herself for so long against forming attachments. Against remembering the good things about Eden Bay. Like the friends with whom she'd giggled and in whom she'd confided. The thing she couldn't get over was the lack of censure in their expressions and their voices today. Were they really willing to accept her without explanations?

Carolee turned down the volume of the radio and glanced at Annie. "So? Are you still speaking to me?"

"You know I never would have gone if you'd told me your plan."

Carolee grinned mischievously. "That's exactly why I kept you in the dark." Another mile passed before she continued. "They were all so excited to hear you were back. Of course there will be some people who will want to hear all the particulars of your mysterious disappearance, but you don't owe them an explanation. Friends accept you just as you are, where you are."

"I had no idea that…that…"

"We cared so much?" Carolee finished for her. "Well, get used to it, sweetie. We're none of us going anywhere. And we all hope you're not, either."

"I don't know what to say. Everyone was so welcoming, so…fun."

"Bet you haven't had a whole lot of that in the past few months."

"Try past few years."

Carolee reached over and patted her arm. "Let us help, Annie. We gals are an awesome force when we put our minds to something."

"I don't know how to thank you."

"Don't worry. Your time will come to help us. With friendships, what goes around, comes around, don't forget."

When she pulled up in front of the cottage and set the brake, Carolee leaned over and hugged Annie. "Now, what do you say? How's about a girls' night out next Friday?"

Annie wanted to say yes, yet her fear of exposure in public places stopped her. But then an idea came to her. "For this first time, what would you say to coming here? I'll fix some chowder, ice down a few beers."

Carolee's eyes shone like a mother whose daughter has just performed an exquisite ballet solo. "Perfect," she said. "I'll tell the others. Seven o'clock okay?"

Annie nodded. "Just right."

Until she made it into the house and thought of Kyle, everything had been just right. She set down her purse and went to the upstairs bedroom where Pete's letter lay open on the bedside table. She let her eyes sweep over the message on the back. "Try my buddy Kyle…you won't find anyone better to love."

In fairness, she owed Kyle a chance to explain why he'd withheld the letter from her. She held it against her heart and, with her eyes closed, spoke to Pete. "I've spent the last week remembering and loving you, darling Pete, but I know I have to set the past aside and replace our dreams with others. If you think Kyle might be part of that plan, well, then…I'll do my best to give him a chance."

This time when she looked at the letter, she nodded in slow recognition, then folded it carefully and tucked it away in her jewelry case. Geneva could have sold the cottage at any point in the past few years. Instead, she had left her this legacy. It was time to do what both her Auntie G. and Pete had encouraged her to do—live.

KYLE PARKED his truck at the curb in front of the Nemecs' house and sat without moving. Never—not even after he had set Rosemary straight—had he experienced such a dread of seeing them. Reluctantly, he stepped out of the cab. It was a beautiful Oregon evening. The faint scent of roses, emanating from Janet's flower garden, made him sad. Pete had often picked a single one of these roses to take to Annie.

Oh, yeah. I really need to think of her right now.

He squared his shoulders and strode to the front door. Bruce greeted him and ushered him to the family room at the back of the house. "Beer? Cocktail?"

"Just a soda, please." This was not a social occasion,

and Kyle was so nervous he didn't know if he could even swallow.

While Bruce put ice in a glass and poured the soda, Kyle wandered to the window. The patio table was set with yellow and red place mats, and a bouquet of spring flowers served as the centerpiece.

Bruce handed him the soda, then laid a hand on his shoulder. "How do you want to do this, son?"

Kyle appreciated the man's sensitivity. "I think it's best before dinner."

"Rosemary and Janet are in the kitchen. Margaret and Rick will be here as soon as the babysitter arrives. What do you say we watch the tail end of the Mariners game while we wait?"

Although Kyle's eyes were fixed on the television set, if he'd been asked, he couldn't have told a thing about the strike count, the number of outs, even the score. The waiting was hell, so he was almost relieved when the Bairds finally arrived and Bruce assembled everyone. Margaret gave him a cursory greeting, then turned away. Rosemary nodded, uncharacteristically quiet. Janet sat next to Kyle on the sofa and the rest found places around the room. Bruce perched on the arm of Rosemary's chair. The term *hot seat* swam up from Kyle's subconscious.

Bruce began. "Kyle came to see me Friday and said he had something he wanted to visit with us about. I'm as in the dark as the rest of you, but I'm sure he wouldn't have asked for this time with us if he hadn't felt it was important."

Silence fell, and Kyle knew it was up to him to fill

the void. "Thank you for being here. I'm not looking
forward to what I have to say to you. It's been a long
time coming and I wouldn't blame you for wondering
why I've waited. All I can say is that I've struggled with
a lot of stuff since Pete died, trying to make sense out
of what happened and my role in it.

"Pete was the brother I never had." Here he had to
clear his throat. Images of Pete filled his head, affect-
ing his concentration on the carefully prepared speech.
He gripped his knees, wondering how to utter the next
words. He didn't dare to look at any of them. "Before I
go on, there's one thing you should know." He raised his
head. "I would gladly have taken that sniper's bullet for
him if I could have. What I came to tell you is this. I'm
responsible for Pete's death."

Bruce stood in protest. "Kyle, no, son. It was a
result of war."

"Please, sir. Let me finish." Clasping his hands
between his knees to conceal their trembling, he went
on. "That day in Afghanistan was bitter cold. Overcast.
Work on the bridge we were building was slow going,
but vital for keeping our supply lines open. We knew
there were guerrillas all over the place, hiding in the
mountains, blending in with the locals. There were tribes
that wanted us gone—at any price. I knew the danger.
As the Humvee driver, it was my job to get the guys out
of there as quickly as possible. But I made two mistakes."

He rose and, like a caged animal, paced back and
forth in front of the fireplace. "First, I was in a hurry to
get back to camp. I warmed up the engine and then let
my attention wander to the mountains, which, even in

that hostile environment, were beautiful. I should have seen movement, sensed the presence of the sniper.

"Second, and far worse, I should have pulled Pete into the cab. That time I let him pause to look at Annie's photo was the split-second difference."

He heard a muffled snort from Margaret. The look on her face revealed more than her mumbled words. "It figures. Annie again."

Kyle stood stock-still, facing the Nemec family. "Pete would still be here if I had done my job."

Janet uttered a sharp cry and then came to stand beside him. She picked up his hands and looked him straight in the eye. "It wasn't your fault, Kyle," she said in a firm voice. "You have to believe that."

Rosemary hugged herself, studying the floor. Rick put an arm around Margaret and shook his head sadly. When Janet dropped Kyle's hands and resumed her seat, he dared to look at Bruce. The man's jaw was working and his eyes were moist. Unable to speak, he merely nodded at him to continue.

"But that wasn't the only time I failed Pete," Kyle said, his voice ragged with emotion. "When Annie ran away, I should have encouraged him to find her. There wasn't much we could do from Guard training, but when we got back to Eden Bay, I told him stuff like 'No girl is worth it' and 'She punted you, man. Forget her.'" Cringing inwardly, he wondered if his own feelings for Annie had motivated those remarks.

"But Pete didn't hear any of that. Loyalty was his middle name. Besides, he was crazy for her. If only I'd helped him more when he was searching so frantically for her, maybe we'd have found her and he wouldn't have been looking at that damned photograph."

His voice broke then. "I'm sorry, so very sorry." He swallowed the sobs thrusting up from his chest. "I'll understand if you don't want me around."

Bruce crossed the room and enveloped him in a bear hug. "We've lost one son. We don't want to lose another." When he stepped back, he sought Kyle's eyes. "It was war, Kyle. Unspeakable things happen in war. There isn't anything much worse than losing a child that way. But we have nothing to forgive, son. No one in this room holds you responsible in any way. Please don't torture yourself."

"Why not?" The bitter question caused everyone to face Margaret. "It has to be somebody's fault."

Bruce moved closer toward his daughter. "Margaret, it's time to quit trying to assess blame. It's time, as well, to move on. Pete's death ravaged all of us. But it was an accident, sweetheart, an accident. Any error in judgment, if that's what we can call it, was Pete's."

"But—"

Bruce spread his arms. "Come here, honey."

Margaret collapsed against her father, grief spilling out in tears.

Janet approached Kyle and laid her hands on his shoulders. "Have you been living with guilt all these years?"

He could only manage a nod of the head.

"It's over, then," Janet continued. "Pete wouldn't want you to suffer on his account. He would want you to play all the ball games he can't, to catch your limit of fish for him. To live, Kyle. Each and every day."

He was overwhelmed by their acceptance. "I don't know what to say. I, uh, expected—"

"To be banished?" Smiling, Bruce looked over Margaret's head at him. "Not in my lifetime, son." He stepped back and led Margaret back to Rick before rejoining Kyle. "Now what do you say I give you the beer you really wanted when you came in?"

"You know me too well."

"I hope so. I practically reared you."

"Does this mean we have to accept Annie Greer, too?" Once again they all turned to Margaret, her eyes glittering with pain.

"What's that supposed to mean?" Bruce looked genuinely puzzled.

"Go ahead, Rosemary, tell them."

Rosemary turned a deep fuchsia. "Please, Margaret. It's no big deal."

"To the contrary. I suspect it's a very big deal. First of all Kyle rejected my sister. But to add insult to injury, the very next day she saw him walking on the beach with Annie Greer." She paused before administering the blow. "Holding hands."

Janet turned to Kyle, her mouth forming a perfect O. "Annie?"

Three sets of female eyes pinned him to the wall. "Well," Margaret said, "wasn't it enough to let Pete down without hurting the rest of us with Annie?"

"What can I say? Like you, I was mad as hell at Annie for disappearing and breaking my buddy's heart. When she came back to Eden Bay, I never wanted to see her. But my work for Geneva Greer made that impossible. I told Annie exactly how angry and disappointed I was about her actions."

"But?" Janet encouraged him to go on.

"She was dealing with quite a bit with her great-aunt. Besides, I kept remembering how much Pete loved her. If he'd been here, he would have comforted her, eased the way. I don't know, I guess I just sort of began doing for her what I thought Pete would've done."

"How gallant," Margaret muttered, swiping at her tearstained cheeks. "And self-serving."

Kyle felt his ears burning. He was sorry for Pete's sister, but he'd had enough of her sarcasm. "Margaret, I regret that you feel so strongly about Annie. You loved Pete and I get it that you never wanted anyone to hurt him, least of all the girl he loved with all his heart. But Annie has her reasons for what happened. Maybe they're none of our business, but that's no reason to hate her. You all liked her before, welcomed her into your home, almost like a daughter. Would Pete want you to ostracize her now?"

Margaret had the grace to shut up and stare at the floor.

Janet took command of the tense situation. "I think we've all said enough for now. Kyle has given us a lot to think about. None of us wants to say anything more right now, anything that might be hurtful." She gazed around the room, fixing her eyes on each of them. "So…let's move outside and get those burgers cooking."

Kyle murmured his excuses to Janet. No way could he gather with them around their table as if nothing had happened. He was on his way to the door when he heard footsteps behind him. Rosemary had followed him. "Kyle?"

He turned and saw gentle acceptance in her expression.

"About Annie...well, I just wanted to say, I'm okay that things didn't work out between us. I've thought a lot about it. I was trying way too hard." She rubbed a hand up and down his arm. "You were right in there. About Pete. About how much he loved Annie. So...if you want to be Annie's friend, or more, I think Pete would approve."

Then she stood on tiptoe and kissed his cheek. "You're a good man, Kyle Becker," she said as she opened the door for him. "There will be other nights for supper."

He walked slowly down the walk, undone by her understanding. How could he tell her that he'd ruined his chances with Annie? That even with Pete's blessing, Kyle would never have a life with the woman he loved.

ON HIS WAY HOME, Kyle stopped at the grocery store to grab a TV dinner or two. It would be a far cry from burgers on the grill, Janet's famous potato salad and Margaret's signature baked beans. He'd never gone away hungry from the Nemecs'. When he was a kid, Janet would even wrap up homemade cookies for him to take home with him.

No cookies tonight. Only rioting emotions. He was humbled by the generosity of Bruce and Janet, their willingness to forgive him. He wondered, though, if they really understood the extent to which he blamed himself.

On the drive home, he thought a lot about Annie. The atmosphere in the Nemec family room had turned stormy when Margaret confronted him. It was almost as if in her eyes the ultimate betrayal had not been dereliction of duty in Afghanistan but his betrayal of Pete with Annie. Yet support for his relationship with Annie had come from the unlikeliest source—Rosemary.

When he pulled into his driveway, he shut off the motor and turned to Bubba. "Go figure, fella. I haven't lost my job. And most of the Nemecs still accept me. I guess it's a good thing Annie's turned her back on me, because the one sore spot with Janet and Margaret, at least, is Annie's treatment of Pete." He plucked the key out of the ignition and opened the door. "They'll never understand without knowing the truth and it's not for me to tell them."

Inside, he stripped off the pressed khakis and sport shirt and exchanged them for a pair of shorts and a gray T-shirt. He flipped on ESPN and grabbed a beer. The running commentary on the tube might as well have been white noise, though, for all the attention he was paying.

If he hadn't given Annie the letter, maybe he'd have had a chance with her. But then, he'd always played second banana to Pete. It seemed the ultimate irony that the one woman he had found to love was still carrying a torch for the one man who'd always overshadowed Kyle. He ached with the need to jump in his truck, drive to the Greer cottage, swoop Annie into his arms and make passionate love to her.

Fat chance of that. Even if she welcomed him, she'd be spooked by any physical affection. Here he was, hard just thinking of her, with less than a snowball's chance in hell of ever holding her again, much less making love to her.

It had been a hell of a day, and he wasn't looking forward to a sleepless or nightmare-ridden night. Finally he stirred and, giving in to hunger pangs, nuked a TV dinner, which turned out to be just as tasteless as it looked.

He was finishing the minuscule cherry cobbler and watching the final inning of a Padres game when a knock sounded on the door.

Nobody ever came to visit him. Not on a Sunday night. Maybe, after thinking about things, Bruce had reconsidered and was coming to have the difficult discussion of Kyle's future. Or it could be that Margaret wanted to fire one last salvo.

He tossed the dinner into the trash, wiped his mouth on a napkin and went to the door. When he opened it, he stared stupefied. What was Annie doing here? For one fleeting moment, he allowed himself to hope.

"Kyle?" She looked so tentative, even childlike, her body swathed in a flannel shirt that fell nearly to her knees. Jeans and running shoes that had seen better days completed her outfit.

"Hey, I guess you found me." He didn't know what she wanted. Didn't know what to say.

"You gave me your card, remember? You're not hard to find."

"Is something wrong?"

"I don't know yet. That's what I came to find out."

He thrust his hands into his pockets to keep from pulling her into his arms. "I've missed you." Damn it, where had that come from? "I thought maybe you didn't want to talk to me."

"For a while I thought so, too."

"And now?"

"Now I need to talk." She cocked her head and peered around his shoulder into the living room. "Uh, do you think I could come in?"

"Sure. Sorry, I forgot my manners." He stood back and let her enter. Bubba, roused from the kitchen floor, ran excited circles around Annie. "Looks like he's glad to see you."

She knelt down, gratifying Bubba with a good ear scratching. Then Kyle heard her say, "I was kind of hoping someone else might be glad to see me."

He lifted her to her feet by the elbow, then said softly, "Someone else is, Annie Greer."

CHAPTER TWELVE

NOW THAT SHE WAS HERE at Kyle's house, Annie found herself at a loss for words. The big-screen TV, a golf bag standing in the corner, oversize furniture, the faint, musty smell of athletic socks—it all screamed "man" in a way that was both intimidating and exciting. Kyle's space. When he'd come to the door in a formfitting shirt and shorts that revealed well-toned legs, her mouth had gone dry and she'd thought about beating a hasty retreat. The decision to come here had seemed simple, even obvious, when she'd contemplated it from the safety of Auntie G.'s armchair. The reality was different—scary in a giddy sort of way.

Kyle swept the Sunday papers off the sofa. "Please sit down and excuse the mess. Can I get you some coffee? Soft drink?"

"This isn't exactly a social call."

His face fell momentarily, and she realized she'd sounded abrupt. He sat at the other end of the sofa. "What kind of call is it, then?"

"I guess it's a clear-the-air visit."

"About…?"

"Pete's letter."

He slumped. "I see. You said some pretty strong things the other night about trust. You were right. I betrayed both Pete's and yours by hanging on to the letter as long as I did."

Before she let him off the hook, she wanted the truth. "It's not like you to do that. I need an explanation, Kyle."

"And you deserve one." He turned toward her, his arm resting on the sofa back. "But you're not going to like everything I have to say."

"Try me."

"Pete was devastated when you left town without so much as a phone call. He nearly drove himself crazy trying to figure out what he'd done to drive you away—"

"Oh God." It had never crossed her mind that Pete would blame himself for her departure.

"He was beside himself, Annie. As soon as he could, he tried to pick up your trail. Your stepfather was no help, for reasons I now understand. The agent at the bus station said you'd bought a ticket for Sacramento, but nobody knew anything more. Pete quizzed everybody he could think of, but no one could tell him a thing. He even tried getting your great-aunt's address abroad from her attorney, but he'd been instructed not to give it out. Pete was like a crazy man. It was as if you'd dropped off the face of the earth. You understand this was my friend, and he was in hell."

"You had every right to be furious." Her hands clenched at her sides, Annie waited for the next blow to fall.

"So far as I was concerned at the time, you had single-handedly destroyed the Pete I knew. No way could any of us understand his devotion to you. Nothing anybody said or did could shake his love for you. He was the most stubborn guy I've ever met where you were concerned. At times, it felt like there was no longer room in his life for me or his family or…for anyone. Except you, and you were a ghost. How could I not be hurt and angry?"

"So I became the target of your rage."

"Big-time. Then when Pete died looking at your photo, in my mind, it was almost as if you'd pulled the trigger."

She doubled over, clutching her sides, moaning.

"I don't want to hurt you like this, Annie, but if I'm to be totally honest, the truth is that I hated you from the moment you left Eden Bay, and it only intensified after Pete got shot."

She cleared her throat and finally found her voice. "You loved Pete. Your feelings are understandable."

"When you showed up at the cottage after all these years, you were the last person I wanted to see. Frankly, I was afraid of what I might do or say. The only reason I agreed to take on the work for Auntie G. was because I could see how important it was to her to have the job done properly."

Annie dared to look at him. "What made you start helping me? Like that day you followed us to the doctor's office?"

"I don't know exactly. You looked so vulnerable trying to get your great-aunt settled in the car. I couldn't help asking myself what Pete would've done. What he would have me do. Caregiving is tough, and I could see how much you loved your aunt. I wanted, somehow, to ease your burden. And that's when things began to change."

"What do you mean?"

"I fought it, but I couldn't hate you any longer, Annie. In fact, I began to hate myself."

"Hate yourself? Why?"

"The anger I bore toward you all those years was misdirected. You were my scapegoat. And then after Pete died…" He raked fingers through his hair and blew out a long breath. "My job was to spot that sniper. Take him out. That would've kept Pete safe." Kyle's face was drawn, the expression in his eyes bereft.

The full impact of what he was saying slowly dawned on her. "Wait. You mean you've blamed yourself for his death?"

"Every day."

"Oh, Kyle." She wanted to reach out to him, to soothe him, but she knew it wasn't the time, that he would not welcome her touch. "It wasn't your fault."

"That's what everyone tells me." He shook his head in disbelief. "You don't blame me?"

"No one could've prevented what happened."

In her eyes, he read forgiveness. A weight rolled off him. "Some friend I am, though. Now I want to steal his girl. Maybe that was always part of it."

He spoke so quietly, at first she thought she'd misunderstood him. "What did you say?"

"That's the main reason I couldn't give you the letter." She waited for him to go on, her heart thudding. "At first I told myself it was because you didn't deserve it. But it was much more than that. I was afraid to compete with your memories of Pete. I didn't know what was in the letter, but I knew whatever it was would come between us. And it has."

"Are you saying that you kept the letter from me because you thought I'd reject you?"

At last he picked up her hands and held them gently in his. "You probably don't know this, and I've only recently been able to admit it to myself, but I've loved you since I was sixteen years old."

"Kyle—"

"Please, let me finish. Before I lose my nerve. All that anger that tied me in knots? It was also about wanting you and feeling so damned guilty about my feelings. What you had with Pete was special, enviable. What kind of friend covets his best friend's girl? But I did." His eyes found hers. "I still do, Annie."

There was no premeditation. As if it was the most natural act in the world, she moved into his arms. Cupping his jaw in her hands, she searched his face for answers. "All this time? Even in high school?"

"You never guessed? Even that night on the beach?"

"I thought what happened was simply the emotion of the moment, but afterward I felt guilty wondering if I'd done something to encourage you." She hesitated, lost in thought. "I still find what you're telling me difficult to believe."

"There's never really been anyone else. You can't imagine how hard I tried to hide it. I even tried to convince myself that I loved you because Pete did and not for myself. When you came back to Eden Bay, I knew I was in trouble."

"Oh, Kyle," she said, drawing his face closer and kissing him, at first tenderly, and then with all the pent-up emotion of long weeks—even years—of denial. She couldn't get enough of the taste of him, the warmth of his skin, the tantalizing way his hand played over her back. It was as if some other woman had temporarily slipped into her body—someone uninhibited, open, quivering with need. The miracle was that he seemed as lost in sensation as her, deepening the kiss, pulling her even closer, as if he would never let her go.

Abruptly, he broke the connection, holding her at arm's length. "We have to stop."

She picked up one hand and kissed it. "Why?"

"Because you're driving me wild, that's why."

"So?"

"Annie, I know you think this is what you want. But you're vulnerable. I couldn't bear to hurt you."

She sat back, holding his hand in her lap. "You think I'm not ready."

"Yeah, I guess. I mean, I don't know, but…"

She felt blood pooling in secret places within her. Yet at the same time, she understood what made him hesitate. What if she had a flashback in the middle of lovemaking? Or froze again? She knew the possibility was there, yet she didn't want to turn back now. If she did…what then? This was Kyle. Dear, dear Kyle, who treated her like a piece of fragile bone china. She moved closer, laying her head against his chest. "There can never be the perfect first time. But if there is, it will be with you. Tonight." She moved her lips across the throbbing artery in his throat. "I want this. I want you."

He moved his head to look deeply into her eyes. "Are you sure?"

"I'm sure."

He scooped her up in his arms and carried her to the bedroom, kicking the door open and depositing her on his bed. She heard him mutter, "Bubba, get lost," when the dog tried to follow them.

Kyle lay down beside her, still fully clothed, and in the dim light shining in from the living room, she saw his tentative, wondering smile, watched while he explored her face with his fingers and then, between kisses, slowly unbuttoned her shirt. "I'll be gentle, Annie," he whispered, "but being here like this, with you, I'm on fire."

When he parted her blouse and unhooked her bra, she realized she had tensed, anticipating his fingers on her breasts. For an instant, the blackness of that long-ago night descended. She took a deep breath and made herself open her eyes and focus on Kyle, a man who would never harm her. Slowly he removed her shirt and bra and set them aside. Her nipples puckered with exposure to the cool air. Still, Kyle didn't touch her there. Instead, he kissed her lips, her forehead, her eyelids, her throat. Then, as if her hands had a mind of their own, she cradled his head and directed him to her breasts. He didn't hurry, but lingered and, with each touch, she found herself increasingly aroused.

When he slipped his hand beneath the waistband of her panties, she flinched involuntarily. He paused. "Too much?" he whispered.

She drew a deep breath. "Just give me a minute."

"Slow and easy, darlin'." He laid a trail of kisses from her neck to her abdomen to gentle her. "We have all night."

Then she felt his fingers plying magic and, shuddering with a fierce, spontaneous need, she writhed beneath him. She sensed in him an urgency he was doing his best to tame. As he buried his head in her neck, his body straining above her, in one blinding moment, she knew that all she wanted in the world was to give herself to him, totally.

Afterward she couldn't remember when their clothes had ended up on the floor or how long she had floated in a daze of exquisite foreplay. She only knew that Kyle had entered her with an almost reverent tenderness and brought her to life again. It was an exorcism that left her trembling with rekindled sexuality and passion for this man who had suffered so long in silence and who deserved to be loved as completely as he had loved her.

For long moments, they lay naked, facing each other, gently exploring curves, flesh, muscles, their gazes locked in a depth of understanding that moved Annie to happy tears. She loved everything about him—his square, capable hands, the scar on his left shoulder, the fine sandpaper of his beard beneath her fingers, the mingled smells of sea-breeze cologne and sex. Nothing this night had been about exploitation or selfishness. Only tenderness and intimacy.

Finally, he pulled up the sheet and brought her into his embrace. "Are you okay?"

"Mmm. Better than okay." She kissed the soft spot beneath his ear. "Thank you, Kyle. I feel so…free."

"You have no way of knowing how long I've dreamed of having you here in my bed. I promise to continue taking it slow."

She curled her fingers against his neck. "Someday I hope—"

"Never mind about someday. Right now, Annie, I'm as happy as I've ever been in my entire life."

She sighed contentedly. "I'm glad. Do you think you could keep on holding me for a while?"

He chuckled against her ear. "For as long as you want, my love."

KYLE FELT something tugging at the sheet. He rolled over and propped up on one elbow. Bubba was insistent. "Easy, boy," he said, rubbing his eyes. He could swear he smelled coffee and bacon.

Then he remembered. Annie. Shooting out of bed, he stepped into clean shorts and pulled on a T-shirt. Glancing in the mirror, he noticed a honker of a grin spreading across his face as memories of the night swept over him. God, she was fantastic. How long had she been up? He glanced at the bedside clock, surprised to see it was after seven.

He ran a hand over his hair, then stepped into the kitchen. "Hey, you," he said, gathering Annie in his arms.

Holding a spatula in the air, she let him dance her around the room. "Careful. You'll get egg on your shirt."

"A small price to pay for having a beautiful short-order cook in my kitchen." Her hair was damp, her cheeks rosy. "You showered already?"

"Sure. You were dead to the world."

He grinned wickedly. "There's a very good reason for that condition, ma'am."

"I couldn't sleep a wink."

Guilt washed over him. "Why not?"

"I couldn't stop thinking about you. About how we got together." She turned aside to flip the bacon. "And especially about how you made me feel whole again. Like a woman."

"*Like* a woman! You are a woman." He came up behind her and put his arms around her waist. "I always knew that beneath all that baggy clothing was not just any woman, but a gorgeous one."

She leaned back against him. "You make me feel safe."

The thought jumped to his mind that he didn't want to make her feel safe. He wanted her to feel sexy. Before he could joke about it, though, he recognized the compliment he'd just been paid. She hadn't felt safe since her stepfather raped her. Until now. "Good," he whispered. "I hope you always feel that way."

Bubba came and stood beside them, brushing against Kyle's leg. He stepped away and pulled dog food from under the counter. "I haven't forgotten you, buddy. But today, somebody else comes first. I hope you approve."

Bubba wagged his tail enthusiastically.

"What time do you go to work?" Annie asked.

"Before now." He found himself grinning again. He just couldn't help it. "But today I'm going to be late."

While she finished preparing breakfast, he took a quick shower, decided to forgo shaving and came back just in time to eat. He ran a hand over his beard. "Hope you don't mind the scruffy pro-quarterback look."

While they ate and made small talk, the air was fraught with sexual tension and unasked questions—as if they couldn't wait to go back to bed but were too shy to put a voice to their desire.

When they'd finished the dishes and were ready to leave the house, he put his arms around her. "So am I forgiven?"

"For what?"

"For holding back on giving you the letter?"

She kissed him lightly. "You had good reasons."

He sobered, his heart pounding. "Annie, I love you so very much."

"I know," she whispered. "And I, you." When she stepped away, she pulled an envelope from her pants pocket and set it on the counter. He recognized it. Pete's letter. "I wasn't sure at first if I ever wanted you to read this, Kyle. But now I do."

"What changed your mind?"

She grazed a hand over the words *For Annie* before turning back to him. Her eyes were sad, but also luminous. "Because I realize now that Pete wrote the letter to both of us." Pulling her keys out, she kissed him again and slipped out the door.

He stood rooted to the spot, unable to grasp the enormity of what she had just done. The letter was hers. Surely Pete had never intended it for anyone else's eyes. Reading it would be intruding into Pete and Annie's sacred space. He crossed to the counter and picked it up, holding it in his hands as if the mere heft of it would direct him.

Bubba stood by the door expectantly. It was past

time to leave for work. Too bad, Kyle thought, slumping onto a kitchen stool and inhaling a cleansing breath. Okay, then. He extracted the letter from the envelope, his face flushing with the shock of seeing Pete's familiar handwriting covering the page. Once more the notion came to him that he was trespassing on intimate secrets. Yet he was pulled into the prose just as if Pete were speaking to him.

...I can barely stand the thought that I will never see you again, that we will never be together as we'd always planned... I don't have a clue how I know, but I just do—you're out there somewhere and you've never stopped loving me.

Kyle could scarcely breathe, the awful reality of Pete's death shocking him all over again. He rubbed his eyes and forced himself to continue.

...We had such plans. How we'd marry and have children. How we'd introduce them to the miracle of tide pools, coastal forests and mountains. How we'd never let one day pass without telling them how much we loved them.

Pete had loved the out-of-doors. Kyle closed his eyes. Eerily, the smell of wood smoke and the sound of rushing water came to him as if he were standing in a mountain grove beside a tumbling stream. He remembered then— the camping trip in the Cascades the two of them had taken just before football practice began their senior year. How excited they'd been about being top dogs. How unabashedly Pete had shared his feelings for Annie.

The final paragraph of Pete's letter, beginning with the harsh words *But I'm gone* nearly did Kyle in. And then came the part about dreams. He didn't know if he could even continue reading. Finally he gathered his courage.

…More than anything, that's what I want for you—dreams. A good man to love and who will love you. Someone who will make you laugh, who will hold you close each night, who will give you children and grow old with you.

Damn it, Pete. It was supposed to be you. Kyle buried his head in his hands, the old guilt washing over him. He'd just made love to Annie, the woman he had adored since he was a kid. How, for even one minute, could he think he should be the someone to make Annie laugh, to give her children, to love her into her golden years?

But, God help him, he wanted to be. What would Pete think of him?

After long minutes he roused himself. It was when he picked up the letter to put it back in the envelope that he noticed the P.S. on the back of the page. As he read the words that sounded so like Pete, he convulsed with grief, shedding all the wild tears he had bottled up for years. *God, Pete, how did you know?*

…Hey, if you don't have anyone particular in mind, I'll make a suggestion. Try my buddy Kyle.

He needs a good woman, and you won't find anyone better to love.

The words swam on the page. Had Pete paused at his car on that long-ago starry night, turned for one last look at the ocean and seen Kyle draw Annie into his arms? Had he suspected Kyle suffered in silence, aching for love of his girl? The answers had died with Pete, but forgiveness was etched in the haunting P.S.

ALL THAT DAY Annie floated around the cottage, unable to settle to work. She felt alive in a strange, new way. Her body tingled with the afterglow of lovemaking, and for the first time in years, she dared to envision a hopeful future. Over and over she replayed his words: *I've loved you since I was sixteen years old.* She had never dared to think about finding love again, but she had discovered it in the most unexpected place of all—Eden Bay.

The week passed in a blur. Days were devoted to work. To her surprise, on Wednesday the owner of the Scottsdale boutique called with exciting news. She was opening a second store in Santa Fe and wanted to feature Annie's signature line of purses in both locations. "You are very talented, Ms. Greer," the woman said just before she concluded the phone conversation.

In the midst of her euphoria, Annie felt Auntie G.'s approving presence filling the house, as if she were clucking, *This is everything I'd hoped for you, petunia.*

Evenings she'd spent with Kyle. He'd stayed over only once, but, oh, that once. To the music of the surf kissing the beach below, they'd made slow, luxurious love. Early that next morning, they'd wrapped up in blankets and taken their coffee out onto the porch. As the sun rose, they listened, without speaking, to a world coming alive with the sounds of stirring birds and animals. Annie snuggled into the curve of Kyle's arm, smiling to herself. It was so beautiful here.

As if reading her mind, Kyle had kissed her forehead and whispered, "How can you leave all of this? Please, Annie, stay in Eden Bay."

She knew he wanted an answer. It was on the tip of her tongue to give him one. She was ecstatically happy. Yet she'd learned not to trust happiness. In the blink of an eye, it could all be taken away. It was best not to make such an important decision under the influence of a perfect sunrise and a body flushed from passion. "I'm thinking about it," she murmured, knowing in her heart that if she lived her dream as Pete had suggested in his letter, she would stay. But there was still the element of fear. In this place, could she ever be free of the shame of the past? Without Kyle, though, could she ever be free anywhere? As if he had spoken aloud, Pete's words sounded in her head: *Live, Annie, live!*

Everything was pushing her toward staying, until Friday morning, when ugly reality intruded. In preparation for the gals' chowder and beer night at the cottage, Annie went to the supermarket. She was fingering the potatoes in the produce section when a woman sidled up next to her. "Hello, Annie." The voice was not friendly.

Looking up, she saw Pete's sister Margaret, her face a mask. "You're still here, I see."

"Why wouldn't I be?"

"Are you serious? After what you did to my brother? I don't know how you have the nerve to set foot in this town."

Old feelings of shame and guilt rendered Annie speechless.

Margaret was obviously on a roll. "But you aren't satisfied simply to come back. You've set your sights on Kyle. Do you have any idea how you've upset our family?" To Annie's astonishment, the woman's eyes filled with tears. "We loved Pete so much and we miss him terribly. Just when we think maybe we're getting on with our lives, you show up as a constant reminder of what we've lost. I don't know what Kyle is thinking, taking up with you. But I know what I'm thinking. How much longer can you continue to hurt the Nemec family?" Digging into her pocket for a tissue, Margaret walked away, wiping her eyes.

Annie had the impulse to go after her, but she couldn't move, stunned by the attack. And if she did go after her, what would she say? She had no defense, and she was the last person from whom Margaret would welcome comfort. And the truth was Annie understood the source of Margaret's bitterness—deep love and abiding sorrow.

By the time Annie arrived back at the cottage, she knew the answer to Kyle's question. The only way she could stay in Eden Bay was if she summoned the courage to tell the Nemecs the truth about graduation night. She had seen such anguish in Margaret. Annie no longer wanted to contribute to that pain. She didn't know if Margaret or the others would listen, but she had to give them a chance, even if just thinking about such a conversation made her weak in the knees.

CHAPTER THIRTEEN

ANNIE GOT THROUGH the rest of the day by concentrating on preparations for her friends. She had kidded herself into thinking she could have a future in Eden Bay without taking responsibility for hurting Pete. Basking in Kyle's and Carolee's acceptance, Annie had overlooked the others—Margaret and the rest of the Nemecs—for whom she represented only pain.

She did her best to set aside those concerns by focusing on menial tasks, determined not to fall apart.

Mary was the first guest, arriving early to peruse the handbag samples. "These are gorgeous," she said, picking up first one then another. "We'll take all you can spare for the auction." Then she studied Annie, her eyes glowing with appreciation. "Who knew you were such an artist?"

The others arrived shortly after and Mary herded them all upstairs to see Annie's creations. Lindsey and Jill insisted on buying a purse apiece. When Annie tried to give them a discount, Jill hooted. "Are you kidding? I couldn't touch one of these in Portland for this price."

Later they moved to the porch where everyone praised the chowder and claimed to prefer the cottage to a restaurant. Betsy gestured at the ocean view. "Look at that. Annie, I hope you never take this place for granted."

"It's beautiful, isn't it?" Annie said softly, a lump forming in her throat.

Following dinner, conversation drifted to high school reminiscences that ordinarily would have left Annie limp with laughter, but tonight she could barely summon a smile.

Carolee put an arm around Annie after the others had left. "Okay, girl. Something's going on with you. Missing your aunt?"

Annie knew she could seize that excuse and the questions would end there. "Always." Unexpectedly, she found herself confiding in Carolee. "But there's more."

Carolee pulled her chair closer. "I figured. You were quiet this evening. I'm a good listener. And a close-mouthed one."

Slowly, like unknotting a snarled strand of yarn, Annie began. "I had good reasons for leaving Eden Bay. Reasons I'd rather not go into."

"I never doubted that. You wouldn't have walked away from Pete otherwise."

Carolee's understanding broke through Annie's reserve, and she found herself talking about the lonely years in Bisbee and the devastating news of Pete's death, which left her with little reason to return to Eden Bay. "Now, though, I really want to stay here, but I'm not sure I can."

"Oh, Annie, why not? We're all so glad you're back."

"Not everyone."

Carolee raised an eyebrow. "Oh, who might that be?"

"For starters, Margaret Baird. I don't know if she can forgive me. If any of the Nemecs can."

"Margaret loved her brother very much. Sometimes people who can't move beyond their grief find a target for their hurt and anger. Maybe you are Margaret's. She's not a bad person, but I think Pete's death cast a shadow over her life."

"That's just it. I'm a constant reminder of Pete."

"But you're entitled to a life, too. Talk to her, Annie."

"I've already decided to, although who knows how I'll be received."

"Take it one step at a time." Carolee hesitated, as if considering her next words. "Besides, there's Kyle Becker."

"Kyle?"

"Oh, honey, you don't think your relationship is a secret? I heard it from Rosemary's friend at the bank."

Annie jumped to her feet and paced to the railing. Carolee joined her. Neither woman spoke until Carolee said quietly, "It's your life, Annie. Yes, Kyle works for the Nemecs, but maybe you're selling them short. They loved you once, too. If there's some explanation that would help them understand why you acted as you did, it's time to share that information."

"It's so hard," Annie said in a strangled voice.

"Nobody said it would be easy, but don't let the past drive you away. Running never solves anything." She leaned over and kissed Annie on the cheek. "I'm leaving now, sweetie, but let me say this. Don't be too quick to turn your back on a future with a wonderful man like Kyle."

Annie remained on the porch, replaying Carolee's words and willing Geneva's spirit to send a sign telling her what to do.

WHEN KYLE CALLED the next morning to ask about the party, Annie put him off, knowing she couldn't face him until she'd spoken with Margaret. She tried to imagine living here if the Nemecs remained hostile to her, but she loved Kyle too much to put him in that situation—being with her yet loyal to the Nemecs.

She dressed carefully in a pair of navy linen slacks and a matching sweater with a sailor collar. Applying makeup, she did her best to disguise the bags under her eyes. Sleep had eluded her the night before.

Wind whipped the shore as she drove down the Coast Highway. She'd debated calling Margaret, but hadn't wanted to risk the woman's out-and-out refusal to see her. Turning into the Bairds' street, she was relieved to see Rick loading their two kids, dressed in soccer uniforms, into the family van. She slowed, waited for them to drive away, then parked across the street from their house.

Standing on the Bairds' front porch with her heart beating a wild tattoo, Annie rang the doorbell.

Margaret opened the door, dressed in jeans and holding a dustrag. "What are you doing here?"

"Could we please talk? I think it would—"

"We have nothing to say to one another." Margaret started to close the door.

"Wait, please!" Margaret paused and, in that brief

interval, Annie made her case. "You deserve to know why I left Pete after graduation. It's time for the truth."

"I don't know what you could possibly say that would make any difference."

Annie swallowed against the lump in her throat. "I loved Pete. You loved Pete. Surely he would ask you to listen before passing judgment on me."

It took forever before Margaret stepped back and let Annie in. "I'm doing this for Pete, not for you."

In the living room, Annie recognized the sofa and coffee table from the senior Nemecs' family room where she and Pete had spent so much time. Then, as if drawn by a magnet, her gaze lighted on the photographs of Pete. Unable to help herself, she moved to stand in front of them.

Margaret came to Annie's side, focused, too, on the pictures. "You hurt him more than you will ever know."

"I've hurt you, as well. And the rest of your family."

Margaret faced Annie. "Yes, you have."

"There's nothing I can do to make things right. But I owe you an explanation."

Margaret gestured toward the sofa before taking her seat in the wing chair. "I'm listening."

Annie panicked. Now that the time had arrived, she had no idea where to start. Fumbling for words, she said, "I loved Pete with all my heart—I've never stopped loving him. But there were things about me, my life, back then that no one knew. Things I didn't talk about. I couldn't even tell Pete everything."

Pausing to collect her thoughts, Annie noticed that Margaret's rigid posture had relaxed somewhat. "You may remember that my mother died during my junior year in high school and my stepfather cared for me after that."

"The bank president?"

"Yes. And contrary to what most people believed, George Palmer was not a nice man. In fact, he became increasingly affectionate." Annie swallowed hard. "In inappropriate ways."

"And Pete knew this?"

"Not for a long time. I was too ashamed to say anything. I felt dirty. Guilty. I didn't know what to do, where to turn."

"Oh my God, Annie."

"Finally I told Pete a little bit about what was happening. He was furious."

"Of course."

"He said if George laid a hand on me, he would kill him. I believed him." She ran her damp hands up and down her thighs. "I kept thinking I could escape when I went to college. But I waited too long."

"Annie, what happened?"

"On the night of graduation, my stepfather raped me."

Seconds ticked by before Margaret spoke. "I'm at a loss for words. That's horrible." Scrubbing her hands across her face, Margaret sighed. Then she crossed the room and sat at the other end of the sofa. "Pete knew?"

Annie shook her head. "I couldn't tell him. I was afraid for him."

"You thought he might actually kill George?"

"Or that he would stay home from his National Guard training and risk his future to protect me. Serving his country was Pete's dream. How could I stand in the way of that?"

"So you left."

"I left."

"But why didn't you get in touch later?"

"I was terrified George would find me. And I knew no one would believe me if I came back to accuse him of what he'd done."

"Pete never quit looking for you."

"So I've heard. I'm so sorry for what I did, but at the time, I thought I had no choice."

Margaret picked up Annie's hand. "These past years must have been painful for you."

Annie nodded. What was there to say?

"Losing Pete was the hardest thing I've faced. And when you came back to town, Annie, emotions I'd thought I had under control resurfaced. It was as if your presence had opened a huge wound."

"It's all right."

"You know, few are so lucky to have had such a wonderful brother." She paused. "I think you're right about what Pete would have done to George. He would never have let anyone hurt you. It will take me a while to process this. But I've misjudged you." She squeezed Annie's hand. "Please forgive me."

Without conscious thought, Annie pulled Margaret into her arms. "And you, me," she whispered.

When Margaret finally sat back, she was smiling through her tears. "I think Pete is very happy today."

It was the best possible outcome. And as Annie perched on a stool at the kitchen counter while Margaret made coffee, it was easy to say, "I need your help with one more thing."

"A talk with Mom, Dad and Rosemary?"

"Yes. They need to hear the truth, too."

"I'd be happy to set up a family meeting. I won't tell them exactly why."

"I'd appreciate that. Would you mind if Kyle was there with me?"

Margaret studied Annie. "So it's that serious?"

Annie blushed, but did not look away. "Yes. I'm in love with him."

Margaret busied herself for several moments. When she spoke, her voice was gentle. "Okay. I know Pete would approve."

And then Annie told her about the letter.

WHEN ANNIE CALLED to invite him for a walk on the beach, Kyle was relieved. He knew the pressure she'd put on herself to entertain Carolee and the others. Before Annie hung up, she added a comment that made him uneasy. "I'm getting close to having an answer for you."

His breath stopped. She had to stay in Eden Bay. Anything else was unthinkable. "There's only one I'll accept."

When he arrived at the cottage, she was dressed in a long-sleeved T-shirt, overalls and pink sneakers. She gave him a brief hug, then grabbed a ball cap. With her ponytail stuck through the band, she looked like the bat girl she'd been for his high school team. He loved everything about her, from the freckles lightly dusting her nose to the green flecks in the hazel of her eyes. "Let's go," he said, taking her hand.

For a few minutes they walked saying nothing. "I think the party went well," she said. "I'm sorry I didn't know Carolee better in high school. She's been a true friend these past few weeks."

He swung their joined hands high. "One more good reason to stay in Eden Bay. You know I love you, and I'm not prepared to lose you."

"Don't press it, Becker. I have more to do before making any decisions."

"Anything you can talk about?"

"As a matter of fact, yes."

He hoped to God he could interpret her words as encouragement.

"You know how difficult it was for me to come back. The memories, both good and bad, haunt me."

"We can do something about that."

"What?"

"You and I can make our own new memories. Then there's counseling. Have you ever tried that?"

"And relive the whole nightmare?"

"But if it helped you heal…?" He put his arm around her. "I'd be there to support you."

Yes, he would. She knew that. He was steady. And maybe someday she would enter therapy. But she was taking her own steps right now. "I did something big today. I went to see Margaret."

He pulled her close. "Oh, Annie. That must've been incredibly hard."

"I told her everything. It was like a gutting. But I

can't live here unless I make peace with the Nemecs. Not just for your sake, but for theirs...and mine."

They stood quietly for a moment, then she took a deep breath.

"I'm not done. Margaret is arranging a meeting with the Nemecs. I need to tell them." She looked directly at him. "Will you come with me?"

"You know I will." He grazed her cheek with his knuckles. "It might comfort them to know you didn't reject Pete. That you loved him and love him still." He nestled her closer. "They are good people. They've forgiven me. They'll forgive you. Then maybe you can forgive yourself."

The surf roared in her ears. She shut her eyes against the image of George infiltrating her mind. Was she doomed to be a victim, permitting what happened with George to control her life?

With a determined shake of her head, she spread her arms to embrace the Pacific. "I'm here," she shouted, and the weight of her decision took flight.

Kyle gathered her in his arms, an expression of hope on his face. "Does that mean what I think it does?"

She reached up and tangled her fingers in his hair. "I love you, Kyle Becker."

Crushing her against him, he covered her face with kisses. "I will spend my life making sure you never regret this decision." When he found her mouth, electricity fired through her body. Then he whispered in her ear, "What changed your mind?"

"Pete," she answered.

Smiling, he nodded his head. "I understand."

THE NEXT AFTERNOON when Kyle picked up Annie, she wore a green sheath, a seashell necklace and sandals. He smiled to himself. No more hiding behind baggy clothes. As they drove toward the Nemecs', he held her hand, offering her reassurance.

"What time is it?" she asked.

"A little before four."

"Could we make a small detour?"

"Sure. Where to?"

She pointed to a side street that led to the top of a hill. "It's time for me to do this."

When the truck crested the rise, they were at the entrance of the Eden Bay Cemetery. Without a word, he drove through the gates and followed the winding road until he found a parking spot near Pete's grave. "Over there." He gestured in the direction of the headstone. "Do you want me to come with you?"

"Someday. Not today."

He waited as she gathered her courage. Then, as if coming to a decision, she nodded to herself and got out. She took a couple of steps before turning around. "Was there an honor guard?"

Everything about the day they buried Pete came rushing back—the singing of "America," the flag-draped coffin, the rifle salute and the mournful, haunting sound of the lone bugler playing "Taps."

"Yes, Annie. There was an honor guard."

IT WAS QUIET under this tree. Distant traffic noises seemed to belong to another planet. One other time, Annie had attempted this journey but she hadn't been able to do it.

To come here was to admit that he was really gone. Now indisputable evidence stared at her from the headstone: *Peter Nelson Nemec. Beloved son, brother and friend.*

Without conscious thought, she found herself speaking aloud, as if Pete were here. "My love, I had to leave Eden Bay. I couldn't stand the thought of you confronting George. I know I hurt you. I hurt, too. We were meant to be together. But then, I guess you always knew that. And knew that I never stopped loving you and wishing the best for you. I'm sorry it didn't work out for us. I came to say goodbye to you, but I know now that will never happen. So long as Kyle and I remember you, there will be no goodbyes, because you will always be part of us. Thank you for giving him to me."

She moved to the headstone, surrounded by beautiful red roses that filled the air with their fragrance. She bent to touch the name etched in the granite. "Rest in peace, darling Pete." When she straightened, she looked toward the heavens, blue and clear. "Okay, God. I think I get it. Take care of my Auntie G. and Pete."

Slowly she made her way back to the truck, where Kyle stood waiting for her. She stepped into his embrace, knowing there was no need for words.

A dog barked somewhere in the distance and she stepped back. "I'd like to see Pete's family now," she said. He helped her into the cab and they were off to face the final challenge.

KYLE RANG THE DOORBELL. Almost immediately Bruce opened the door. He was more wrinkled and his hair more silver than Annie remembered, but he had the same kind eyes. "Annie, Kyle. Please come in."

The scent of a familiar spicy potpourri took Annie back in time. She had spent hours here with Pete's family—watching TV, playing games, looking at family photos with his mother. In a daze of memory, she let Kyle lead her into the family room, where Janet, Margaret and Rosemary waited. Margaret sent Annie an encouraging smile.

"We're relieved you decided to come, Annie." Janet gestured to the game table. "Have a seat, please. Could I get either of you something to drink?"

Annie declined, even though her mouth was desert dry.

"No, thanks," Kyle said.

"We're interested in listening to whatever you have to say." Although Bruce's tone was conciliatory, Annie noticed both of the senior Nemecs held themselves stiffly.

After they were seated, Kyle broke the awkward silence. "Annie realizes how devastating it was to Pete when she left so suddenly. She knows you must've wondered how she could treat him so callously. But she had a good reason. It's a difficult story, but I think it may help to lay some questions to rest." He turned to Annie and nodded encouragingly.

She felt all pairs of eyes boring into her. She had an overwhelming urge to bolt from the room.

"I can only guess how horrible it was for Pete when I disappeared. I want you to know I would never have hurt him if there'd been any other choice."

"Go on," Bruce said, his face blank.

"I know everyone in town regarded my stepfather highly for all he did for the community. So it would have been incredibly difficult for me to shatter that image. Only Pete knew the truth."

Janet sat forward. "What truth?"

Biting her lip, Annie looked from one person at the table to another. "Late in my senior year, George started abusing me." Once the words left her mouth, it was as if she'd slapped both Nemecs in the face.

"Wait." Bruce shook his head in confusion. "What are you saying? George Palmer?"

"Pillar of the community," Annie said bitterly, the remembered helplessness rising to the surface. "Loving stepfather."

Janet's eyes were round with shock. "Verbally? Physically?"

"No. Sexually."

Bruce buried his head in his hands, and Janet uttered a small cry. When he finally looked up, he said, "And Pete knew?"

"He vowed to kill George if he ever laid a hand on me. I never doubted him."

"Oh God," Janet said. "There's more, isn't there?"

Ducking her head, Annie felt shame reddening her face. In a squeaky voice, she said, "Yes. On graduation night George raped me."

Rosemary uttered a strangled cry, and Bruce leaped to his feet, knocking over his chair. "Goddamn it! That son of a bitch!"

Janet rose to calm her husband. "Let her finish, Bruce, please."

Bruce picked up the overturned chair and slumped back into it. "Annie, I'm so sorry. You must have felt completely alone."

"Except for Pete. But I couldn't tell him. He was leaving for Guard camp and...he'd said he would kill George. I couldn't let that happen."

Janet's eyes filled with tears. "So you left Eden Bay to save him?"

"And to save myself."

"Oh, honey," Janet said, sniffling into a tissue.

Bruce seemed puzzled. "George claimed he tried to find you. Said he hired a private investigator."

Annie choked back a sardonic laugh. "Not likely. It was to his advantage for me to disappear and never return."

"I see that now." Bruce blew out an exasperated sigh.

Annie shifted the subject, anxious to move beyond the specter of George Palmer. "I'm sorry about the way Pete died."

"It was an accident of war," Bruce said in a firm voice. "Pete's death is nobody's fault." He looked from Annie to Kyle. "Both of you have wasted too much time blaming yourselves. Yes, we miss our son, but we don't want you living with regret."

Janet wiped her eyes. "I'm so ashamed. All this time I thought you'd treated Pete shabbily. Please, Annie, accept my apology."

"And mine," Rosemary said, rising to her feet and placing her hands on Annie's shoulders.

"There's nothing to apologize for. How could you have known?"

"Will you stay in Eden Bay?" Janet asked hopefully.

"I'd like to, but I don't want my presence here to cause anyone further pain."

Bruce smiled Pete's lopsided smile. "The only pain you would cause is by leaving."

Janet stood, a loving smile on her face. "I believe there is some champagne chilling in our refrigerator. I can't think of a better reason to open it." Bruce went with her to open the bottle.

Kyle rose and pulled Annie to her feet. "Feel better?"

She nestled against him. "Now I do." She took a cleansing breath. "No one's angry."

Both Rosemary and Margaret laughed, and Margaret said, "I, for one, am tired of being angry."

"Think about it," Kyle said, nodding his head toward the sisters. "This family is a big reason why Pete was such a great guy."

Bruce and Janet came back into the room carrying flutes bubbling with pale champagne. "A toast," Janet said, raising her glass. "To Annie. Welcome home!"

After they each took a sip, Bruce followed suit. "To Annie and Kyle and their future in Eden Bay."

"Here, here," the rest of the Nemecs chorused.

"One more, please." Kyle's expression turned serious. He put his arm around Annie and drew her close. Then he raised his glass. "To Pete."

Annie looked up at Kyle, her heart overflowing with love. Gently, she clinked her glass to his. "To Pete," she echoed.

EPILOGUE

Late September

ANNIE STUDIED her reflection in the full-length mirror. The dress was plain, but classic in its simplicity. The sleeveless, V-necked bodice hugged her breasts, then tapered to her waist and clung to her hips. Just above the knee, the material gave way to gores of embroidered satin. She had never imagined having such a beautiful wedding gown. She touched a hand to her upswept hair, adorned with a coronet of white rosebuds. She hardly recognized the woman looking back at her from the mirror. For so long, she'd hidden her body. It was hard to imagine the glamorous creature in the mirror was the same Annie Greer.

Slowly she pivoted to face her bridesmaids—Carolee, her matron of honor, and Pete's sisters. Their dresses, in variegated tones of sea-green and teal-blue, reminded her of her beloved ocean. "I can't believe it," she murmured. "This is like a fairy tale."

Margaret stepped forward to tuck a lock behind Annie's ear. "We were all due for a happy ending."

Embracing her, Annie whispered, "Thank you so much for loaning me your beautiful wedding dress."

"It was the least I could do after being so bitchy to you."

Smiling, Annie mused to herself about the long way they'd all come in these past few months. She and Kyle had found each other and, with the love and understanding of the Nemecs, had been able to move beyond their shame and guilt.

"Ready?" Carolee asked. "It's almost time."

"Give me a minute." Annie took a tissue and wiped her eyes, trying not to disturb her makeup.

Rosemary touched her arm. "Are you all right?"

"Yes, I'm fine, really. It's just…for a moment there, I felt Pete's presence so strongly." She gazed fondly at each of the women. "He'll always be part of me."

"Of all of us," Rosemary said. "More than anyone, though, he would want you to be happy."

Annie turned to the window, picturing Kyle, appreciating from the bottom of her heart his patience, understanding and huge capacity for love. "I am," she breathed, opening her eyes and facing them again.

Rosemary straightened the hem of Annie's dress. "You're getting a wonderful guy. Remember, I once thought he was the one for me."

Annie smiled at her. She and Rosemary had discussed the issue.

Rosemary continued. "I realized several months ago that Kyle and I were never meant to be. And now—" she winked mischievously "—I'm bringing someone to the reception I want you all to meet."

"A man?" Margaret and Annie shrieked in chorus.

Like a cat licking cream from her whiskers, Rosemary grinned. "You'll see."

Janet and Bruce waited downstairs, and as the four women approached, Janet clapped her hands. "You're all simply breathtaking. But especially the bride." She held out her arms to Annie. As they embraced, Janet uttered words Annie knew she would never forget. "Darling girl, Bruce and I are so blessed to have you back in our lives. We love you."

It was a short drive to the picnic pavilion at the end of the fishing pier. Carolee, Jill, Lindsey, Mary and Betsy had insisted on decorating it with ivy and fresh flowers. At the end nearer the water, they had erected an arbor where the Nemecs' minister stood with Kyle and his groomsmen. A trio of musicians sat to one side. Partly obscuring the setting sun, wisps of coral, mauve and pink floated above the ocean.

They waited as the last of the guests gathered. Exactly ten minutes before the sun was due to slip beneath the horizon, the musicians began playing "You Light Up My Life." Janet walked down the pier and took her seat. To the strains of Pachebel's "Canon in D major," Auntie G.'s favorite, one by one the bridesmaids took their places to the right of the minister. Then it was Annie's turn.

She tucked her arm into Bruce's. He patted her hand. "You've done me a great honor by asking me to give you away."

She stood on tiptoes and kissed his cheek. "You're the closest thing I have to a father. Thank you for loving me."

"Pete wouldn't have it any other way," he said, his voice husky. He cleared his throat. "Now, young lady, let's get this show on the road. This day is for you and Kyle."

Her journey to this moment seemed impossibly long, but so very worth it. Waiting for her was the man Auntie G. and Pete—the two most important people in her past—had selected for her. Kyle Becker, the man who knew her innermost secrets and loved her still. The man who had taught her the most important lesson of all—to live!

"I'm ready," Annie said, with a confidence born of her great love for Kyle and his for her. With her eyes focused on her handsome bridegroom, she took her first step into the future.

* * * * *

*Celebrate 60 years of pure
reading pleasure with Harlequin®!*

*Step back in time and enjoy a sneak preview
of an exciting anthology
from Harlequin® Historical with*
THE DIAMONDS OF WELBOURNE MANOR.

This compelling anthology features three stories
about the outrageous Fitzmanning sisters. Meet
Annalise, who is never at a loss for words... But
that can change with an unexpected encounter in
the forest.

*Available May 2009
from Harlequin® Historical.*

"I'm the illegitimate daughter of notoriously scandalous parents, Mr. Milford. Candidates for my hand are unlikely to be lining up at the gates."

"Don't be so quick to discount your charms, my dear. Or the charm of your substantial dowry. Or even your brothers' influence. There are as many reasons to marry as there are marriages."

Annalise snorted. "Oh, yes. Perhaps I shall marry for dynastic reasons, or perhaps for property or influence. After all, a loveless, practical marriage worked out so well for my mother."

"Well, you've routed me on that one. I can think of no suitable rejoinder." Ned rose to his feet and extended his hand. "And since that is the case, let me be the first to wish you a long and happy spinsterhood."

Her mouth gaped open. And then she laughed.

And he froze.

This was the first time, Ned realized. The first time

he'd seen her eyes light up and her mouth curl. The first time he'd witnessed her features melded together in glorious accord to produce exquisite beauty.

Unbelievable what a change came over her face. Unheard of what effect her throaty, rasping laughter had on his body. It pounded a beat upon his ear, quickly taken up by his pulse. It echoed through him, finally residing in his stirring nether regions.

So easily she did it, awakened these sensations within him—without any apparent effort at all. And she had called him potentially dangerous? Clearly the intelligent thing for him to do would be to steer clear, to leave her to the tender ministrations of Lord Peter Blackthorne.

"You were right." She smiled up at him as she took his hand and climbed to her feet. "I do feel better."

Ah, well. When had he ever chosen the intelligent path?

He did not relinquish her hand. He used it to pull her in, close enough that he could feel the warmth of her. "At the risk of repeating Lord Peter's mistake and anticipating too much—may I ask if you'll be my partner in battledore tomorrow?"

Her smiled dimmed. Her breath came a little faster. His own had gone shallow, as if he'd just run a race—and lost. He ran his gaze over the appealing lift of her brow and the curious angle of her chin. His index finger twitched.

"I should like that," she said.

His finger trembled again and he lifted it, traced the pink and tender shell of her ear, the unique sweep of her jaw. Her pulse leaped beneath her skin, triggering his own. Slowly he tilted her chin up, waiting for her to object, to step back, to slap his hand away.

She did none of those eminently sensible things. Which left him free to do the entirely impractical thing.

Baby soft, the skin of her lips. Her whole body trembled when he touched her there.

He leaned in. Her eyes closed, even as she stood straight against him, strung as tight as a bow. He pressed his mouth to hers. It was a soft kiss, sweet and chaste. And yet he was hot and hard and as ready as he'd ever been in his life.

She drew back a little. Sighed. Their breath mingled a moment before she slowly backed away.

"Oh," she breathed. Her dark eyes were full of wonder and something that looked like fear. He took a step toward her, but she only shook her head. His outstretched hand fell to his side as she turned to disappear into the wood. This was the first time, Ned realized. The first time, since he'd come to the house party at Welbourne Manor, that he'd seen her eyes light up.

* * * * *

*Follow Ned and Annalise's story
in May 2009 in
THE DIAMONDS OF WELBOURNE MANOR.
Available May 2009
from Harlequin® Historical.*

*Available in the series romance section,
or in the historical romance section,
wherever books are sold.*

**We'll be spotlighting a different series
every month throughout 2009
to celebrate our 60th anniversary.**

Look for Harlequin® Historical in May!

Celebrations begin with
a sumptuous Regency house party!

Join three scandalous sisters in

**THE DIAMONDS OF
WELBOURNE MANOR**

Glittering, scintillating, sensual fun
by Diane Gaston, Deb Marlowe
and Amanda McCabe.

**60 years of Harlequin,
600 years of romance
in Harlequin Historical!**

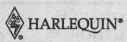
HARLEQUIN®

American ★ Romance®

LAURA MARIE ALTOM
The Marine's Babies

Men Made in America

Captain Jace Monroe is everything a Marine
should be—strong, brave and honorable. He's also
an instant father of twin baby girls he never knew
existed! Life gets even more complicated when he
finds himself attracted to Emma Stewart, his new
nanny. But can this sexy, fun-loving bachelor do
the right thing and become a family man?
Emma and the babies are counting on it!

Available in May
wherever books are sold.

LOVE, HOME & HAPPINESS

You're invited to join our Tell Harlequin Reader Panel!

By joining our new reader panel you will:

- Receive Harlequin® books—they are FREE and yours to keep with no obligation to purchase anything!
- Participate in fun online surveys
- Exchange opinions and ideas with women just like you
- Have a say in our new book ideas and help us publish the best in women's fiction

In addition, you will have a chance to win great prizes and receive special gifts!
See Web site for details. Some conditions apply.
Space is limited.

To join, visit us at

www.TellHarlequin.com.

HARLEQUIN® *Super Romance®*

COMING NEXT MONTH

Available May 12, 2009

#1560 SUMMER AT THE LAKE • Linda Barrett
Count on a Cop
This lakeside cabin is the perfect place for Kristin McCarthy and her daughter to piece together their lives. But with Kristin's distrust of cops, who would have thought one—namely Rick Cooper—would help her daughter heal? Or that Kristin would fall for him?

#1561 HE CALLS HER DOC • Mary Brady
To prove to her hometown that she's good enough to be its doctor, Maude DeVane needs time. And she has it. Until Guy Daley—the doctor she once thought she loved—shows up. She can't seem to avoid him, especially when his niece turns matchmaker!

#1562 THE STRANGER'S SIN • Darlene Gardner
Return to Indigo Springs
Wrongfully accused of a crime, Kelly Carmichael has no choice but to solve the case. That brings her to Indigo Springs and the attentions of park ranger Chase Bradford. A special bond quickly forms between them, but will it survive what they discover?

#1563 THE BOYFRIEND'S BACK • Ellen Hartman
Going Back
As a pregnant teen, letting everyone believe JT McNulty was the father of her child seemed the only answer to Hailey Maddox's predicament. But she never guessed the impact her lie would have. And now, after all these years, JT's come home....

#1564 PICTURE-PERFECT MOM • Debra Salonen
Spotlight on Sentinel Pass
It's a TV plot. What are the odds of Mac McGannon falling for a star like Morgana Carlyle? Yeah, that slim. But it's happening. And he's not the only one. His daughter thinks Morgana is the perfect mom. Just one snag—Morgana is not who she claims to be.

#1565 WEDDINGS IN THE FAMILY• Tessa McDermid
Everlasting Love
On the day of their daughter's wedding, Caroline questions her own marriage to Nick. Facing life's ups and downs, she expected they'd be closer than ever. But he seems so far away from her now. After a lifetime together, can they find the love they once shared?

HSRCNMBPA0409